My darling husba...

What else can hap... ...th our dreams and o... have serious finan... night of the Mardi Gras season—a blackout has hit the French Quarter and surrounding areas. To make things worse, the generator has failed, leaving the Hotel Marchand in utter darkness.

Mother and I are babysitting our beautiful granddaughter Daisy Rose, but the power outage hasn't affected this section of the city. I know our daughters will have everything under control as best they can, but I had to call the hotel for my own peace of mind. Apparently the Twelfth Night party is carrying on as planned. The guests simply danced into the courtyard, taking the festivities out beneath the stars. But the night is still not over, and until the power comes back on, we won't know if any serious damage has taken place.

I'm trying to keep my spirits up, but oh how I wish you were here with me. At least writing to you this way helps me to stay calm.

Ton amour,

Anne

Dearest Reader,

The very first time I became aware of New Orleans, Little Joe Cartwright's mother, Marie, was said to have come from there. I am referring, for those of you who are younger than I am (in fact, but not in spirit), to *Bonanza,* a Western TV show that ran for fourteen and a half years and inspired me to throw myself into writing. Ben Cartwright met and married his third wife in New Orleans. Through his eyes, New Orleans appeared to be a fabulous place with mysterious people and breathtaking architecture. Later, as I watched *Bourbon Street Beat* reruns, I discovered that New Orleans was the home of jazz, the blues and wonderful music. There were other TV series and movies to take me there over the years. Sadly, I never got to see the city for myself before Katrina wreaked havoc on so much beauty and history. Maybe, for me, that is to the good, because in my mind, New Orleans will always remain as gracious, as lovely, as timeless as it always was and I can revisit it anytime I wish. In my heart, I know that the beauty that was will once again return.

With love,

Marie Ferrarella

MARIE FERRARELLA
The Setup

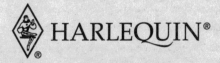

HARLEQUIN®

TORONTO • NEW YORK • LONDON
AMSTERDAM • PARIS • SYDNEY • HAMBURG
STOCKHOLM • ATHENS • TOKYO • MILAN • MADRID
PRAGUE • WARSAW • BUDAPEST • AUCKLAND

Recycling programs
for this product may
not exist in your area.

ISBN-13: 978-0-373-18905-2

THE SETUP

Copyright © 2006 by Harlequin Books S.A.

Marie Rydzynski-Ferrarella is acknowledged as the author of the work.

This edition published by arrangement with Harlequin Books S.A.

® and TM are trademarks of the publisher. Trademarks indicated with ® are registered in the United States Patent and Trademark Office, the Canadian Trade Marks Office and in other countries.

www.eHarlequin.com

Printed in U.S.A.

Marie Ferrarella began writing when she was eleven. She began selling her stories many years after that. Along the way she acquired a master's in Shakespearean comedy, a husband and two kids (in that order) and the dog came later. She sold her first romance novel in November of 1981. The road from here to there has over 150 sales to it. She has received several RITA® Award nominations over the years with one win for *Father Goose* (in the Traditional Category). Marie figures she will be found one day—many, many years from now, slumped over her computer, writing to the last moment—with a smile on her face.

CHAPTER ONE

EMILY LAMBERT STOOD for a moment in the doorway of her father's study. Outside, a bitter January wind was attempting to rattle the windows of the two-story Tudor house. Even for Boston, this year's winter had been particularly brutal so far.

Her father didn't seem to notice the rattling or to be aware of her presence. Given his obvious preoccupation, she had a feeling that she could have stood there for an hour and he still wouldn't have noticed her. Whatever he was working on tonight had captured his attention.

Ordinarily, Emily would have just slipped away again, and waited for a better opportunity, but time was growing short. They were almost down to the wire. She felt a little edgy. Her father was a sweet, kind-hearted man, but he could be incredibly stubborn at times, and she had a feeling this was going to be one of them.

Tossing her straight black hair over her shoulder, she rapped once on the door jamb and waltzed into the room as if she owned it. Sixteen going on thirty, Emily sometimes felt as if she were the parent and her corporate-lawyer father the child. In reality, their relationship was a seesaw of give and take and they were incredibly close. They had been ever since her mother died in a car accident eight years ago. It was then that Jefferson Lambert, the brightest corporate lawyer God ever created, at least as far as she was concerned, had taken over the responsibility of being both mother and father to her while still working full-time at Pierce, Donovan and Klein.

Always busy, he still found time to be there for her whenever she needed him, whether it was to attend a school play, to tutor her in math, or to show her the finer points of tennis. Every moment of his day was accounted for and he had none left over for a social life. In her younger, more self-centered days, this had worked out just fine. She liked having her father all to herself. But now that she was beginning to see boys as something other than the annoying enemy, she really needed her dad's attention to be focused away from her.

A late bloomer, Emily was just barely learning how to make herself desirable to the opposite sex, and she had absolutely no idea what kind of woman her father would like. She was increasingly aware of their own differences in taste, for instance. Her father liked musicals, for heaven's sake, and could quote the lyrics to maybe a hundred songs or more, and each one could send her running from the room.

The very thought of a musical made her want to shiver. She could only pray that somewhere out there was a woman with similar strange tastes.

Emily was determined. She just *had* to get her father back into the dating pool. Of late, it had become her mission in life. She was fairly certain that he would never find anyone if he continued to focus on her and his work. When that invitation from his old fraternity at Tulane University in New Orleans had arrived last year, she'd been overjoyed, positive that her prayers had finally been answered. Or at least addressed. The invitation was for a huge reunion.

Knowing that her father would go solo and probably remain that way, Emily had scraped together every penny she had in order to pay an online dating service to set her father up with a date once he was in New Orleans. With time growing short, she still had to determine which one to use.

All her plans had been unceremoniously upended when her father informed her that he had absolutely no intention of attending the reunion. He'd under-scored his decision by balling up the invitation and tossing it into his wastepaper basket with the finality of a slam-dunk. She'd fished it out the next morning. And then again a few days after that. Each time, she'd smoothed the invitation out and placed it back in the center of his desk—where it was supposed to be now.

Except that it wasn't.

Glancing down, she saw it was in the waste-basket. Emily sighed and bent down to retrieve the paper that represented, she hoped, her first step toward independence.

"You dropped this," she announced cheerfully as she placed the now torn invitation dead center in front of her father.

Jefferson Lambert raised his blue-gray eyes from the computer screen and glanced at the child he thought of as his whole world. At forty-seven, he still looked like he could play a mean game of tennis and not be winded at the end of it—true on both counts. Tall and athletic, he had straight black hair like his daughter. Only the smattering of gray that was beginning to creep in at the temples hinted at the fact that perhaps he was not quite as young as he initially appeared.

Of course, to tease her, he called each gray hair he had "Emily," in honor of the person he claimed to have turned his hair gray in the first place.

"No, I didn't 'drop it,'" he told Emily patiently. "I've already told you. I'm not going to the reunion. I have too much to do here, and besides, it's going to be a huge waste of time."

Time was something Emily felt people had the right to waste occasionally—especially if they spent their waking hours doing things for someone else. Her father needed to do something for himself for a change.

"Dad…" She gave a long-suffering look.

"Emily," he echoed back at her in the same singsong tone she'd used.

Emily frowned. She hated it when he mimicked her, however harmlessly intended, especially when she was attempting to do something for his own good. If that "something" included her own good, well, so much the better. Two for the price of one. But her main concern, at the moment, was getting her father on the right path.

The wind howled, as if adding its two cents. Emily took it as encouragement. "You need to get out, to have some fun for a change."

"I do have fun," Jefferson protested with a trace of humor. "I have fun with you."

"Adult fun," she specified. "Uncle Blake'll be there," Emily reminded him. "Don't you want to see Uncle Blake?"

Blake Randall had been Jefferson's roommate at Tulane. Blake had also been in the fraternity with him. No one who knew them would have pegged them as friends. He and Blake were as different as night was from day. Maybe because of that, they got along well. The two had remained close after graduation—so close that Jefferson had asked Blake to be Emily's godfather when he found out that Donna was pregnant.

Consequently, Blake made it a point to come around during the holidays each year, bringing with him gifts purchased with the sole intention of spoiling Emily rotten. Blake had no family of his own, no long-standing commitments other than to his career. Jefferson thought of him as rootless, and although he really liked the man, he had no desire to live the kind of life Blake lived, even for a weekend.

"We just saw Blake at Christmas, remember?

And I'm sure he'll be back at some point. He's never missed your birthday—by much," he added with a grin. At least when Blake came to Boston, the man was on Jefferson's turf and he could call the shots. He found it saner that way. Back in New Orleans, most likely it would be a case of anything goes. Not Jefferson's style.

Emily rolled her eyes dramatically. Her birthday was in July. It might as well be half a century away as far as she was concerned. She was interested in the here and now. "The world could go up in smoke in another six months, Dad," she protested. "Or be washed away, the way New Orleans very nearly was by Katrina. In case you haven't noticed, these are very fast times we're living in."

Jefferson worked hard at suppressing a smile. "Then maybe some of us should slow down," he said, looking at her pointedly.

"Dad, don't you want a social life?" Emily cried, frustrated. "I'm not going to be sixteen forever, you know. I'm going to have a life, too." And then she added what she felt was her crowning argument. "Someday, I'm going to go off on my own and get married."

Pushing back from his desk for a moment, Jefferson pretended to give his daughter a long, scrutinizing look. "Then I guess I'd better enjoy you while I still have the chance."

He was being extremely difficult, Emily thought, feeling her patience coming to an end. "What are you going to do when I leave home?"

Jefferson sighed soulfully, then assumed a hang-dog expression. "Sit in a rocking chair, wrap myself up in a shawl and enjoy the memories we created when you were sixteen."

Emily threw up her hands. This was pointless. Her father was a wonderful, good man. There was none better and she knew it. But he could be completely inflexible when he wanted to be.

What she needed, she decided, was to bring out the big guns. She needed Uncle Blake.

"I give up," she announced for her father's benefit.

"That's my girl." Tempted to ruffle her hair the way he used to, Jefferson managed to hold himself in check. He missed the contact they used to have, missed the little girl she'd been. But he did his best to respect her boundaries whenever she set them up. "Know when you're out-manned." With a wink, he went back to his work.

She wasn't out-manned, Emily thought, or out-maneuvered. Not yet, anyway.

Moving quickly, she retreated to her room, closed the door behind her and got on her cell phone. There was a phone in her room, but she didn't want to risk getting on the land line. If her father picked up the receiver to make a call, he might overhear her and put a stop to what she was about to do.

Which was get help.

Unlike other times she'd called Blake, it took her only one try to reach him at his home. His booming, cheerful voice as he said hello made her feel that everything was going to be all right. Nothing ever stopped Uncle Blake when he set his mind to do something.

Getting on her bed, she sat down with her legs tucked beneath her and launched into her plan. "Uncle Blake, it's Emily."

"Hey, hi, kiddo. How's the prettiest girl in Massachusetts?"

Emily needed no more of an opening than that. Within the space of a minute, everything came pouring out, one word tumbling over the next. With Blake, she found she could be the exuberant teenager that she couldn't quite be with her father. Blake didn't need looking after the way her father did. With Blake, she didn't have to wear two hats. She could just be Emily.

"Stumped, Uncle Blake. I can't get Dad to go to the reunion."

She heard him laugh on the other end. "Not that I was going to let your dad pass it up, but why's having him attend so important to you, sugarcake?"

Emily saw no reason to fabricate. "I thought that some time away from home might help get Dad to loosen up a little. Learn to have some fun. After all, he's not getting any younger and he needs female companionship before he's too old to attract anyone."

"Ouch."

Emily bit her lip. She hadn't meant to insult her godfather. Older people could be very touchy about their age. "You know what I mean, Uncle Blake.

Dad acts like an old man. I want him to act like you."

"Nice save."

She beamed. "Anyway, I filled out an application for him to a dating service I saw online. I've been saving up so I can send it in for him. I thought if I could arrange for a date for Dad while he's down in New Orleans with you for the reunion, maybe—"

"Hey, hey, slow down, kiddo. Did you say a dating service?"

She didn't know if her godfather would take offense at that. She'd heard it was the way some adults got together because they no longer had the luxury of school as a meeting place.

"Yes," she said, drawing out the word as she waited to see if censure would follow.

To her relief, Blake just laughed. Everything, she thought, was going to be all right. Blake had a way of making things work out.

"Hang on to your money, Em," he advised. "It just so happens that I might know someone who can set your dad up for free."

"Really?" she squealed. It sounded too good to be true.

"Really," he promised her. "Just leave everything to me."

She wanted to believe him, but her father might dig in his heels and then they'd be sunk. And she'd have to put growing up on hold indefinitely. Something she wasn't prepared to do.

"But what if Dad won't go, Uncle Blake? You can't just tie him up and throw him on the plane."

"No need," Blake assured her. "Your father will go to the reunion *and* on the date we set up. Don't worry."

She tried not to. If her godfather said something was going to happen, then it would happen. It was that simple. "Uncle Blake, you're the best."

"Won't get an argument out of me," he chuckled.

Getting off the bed, she began to rummage around on her desk. She'd hidden the form under her World Studies book, fairly confident that her father wouldn't find it there even if he did come into her room while she was out.

Eureka, it was still here, she congratulated herself as she extracted the form from beneath the book. "Okay, I'll fax you his application as soon as I hang up," she promised.

"You actually did fill one out," she heard Blake marvel on the other end.

"Sure, why not?" It seemed like the logical thing to do.

"You're your father's daughter, Em, except a lot prettier," he teased. "Send the fax on over, and I'll see about getting it to that friend of mine. She's in the dating business and I'll ask her if she can rustle up a date for your dad for the reunion."

"She has to be pretty," Emily cautioned quickly. Her father wasn't really into looks, but it would help if his first date in a hundred years was pretty.

"Understood."

She could tell he was about to end the conversation. "And fun," she added quickly.

"Naturally."

What else, what else? she thought, her mind racing. What else did adults value? And then she thought of the boy in her third period bio class. The one who made her breath stop in her lungs. "And sexy."

Blake paused, then recovered and laughed. "How old did you say you were, kiddo?"

She knew he was teasing, but just in case he still thought of her as a little girl, she wanted to set him straight. "Uncle Blake, I'm not a child."

"Nope. Not even children are children anymore," he said with a note of sadness. The world was spinning much too fast. He knew that Jefferson would agree. "Consider your dad spoken for."

"YOU DID WHAT?" Jefferson demanded several days later.

Ordinarily, he didn't raise his voice, didn't believe in it. But this wasn't something that fit under the heading of "ordinary." He stared at his daughter incredulously, waiting for an answer.

On a rare half day off from the firm, he'd come home early to take Emily out for a game of tennis and then perhaps to dinner, if she didn't have too much homework. But before he could make his announcement, Emily had waylaid him in his den. She was holding up one of the portable phones and announcing that "Uncle Blake" wanted to speak with him.

An uneasy feeling had rippled through him, telling him that he was going to be less than thrilled in the next few minutes. The feeling increased when Emily pressed the speakerphone button. Instead of retreating and letting him talk to Blake alone, she'd hurriedly told him the reason for both the call and her excitement.

Faced with their collusion, Jefferson was far from happy. So far that he needed a road map to make his way back.

His eyes darkened, as did his expression.

Emily held fast to her courage. Seeing her father angry was not a common occurrence. The last time he'd looked like this was when her English teacher had given her an unsatisfactory grade that her father felt was purely subjective. Not one to back down when he felt he was right, he'd gone to the school to straighten the matter out and had managed to get a third party to read the essay. Emily's grade had been upped from a C to an A-minus.

That had been good. This, she was worried, might not turn out so well.

She cleared her throat and repeated what she'd told him. "I said Uncle Blake found you a date for when you fly down to Tulane for the frat reunion."

Jefferson ignored the cordless receiver she was holding out to him. "First, I'm not flying down to Tulane for the reunion. We've already been through that," he reminded her. "And second, even if I was going down for the reunion—which I am not—I don't need anyone to find me a date—"

"Well, you certainly aren't finding any yourself, are you, Jeffy?" The voice over the speakerphone interrupted.

Jefferson frowned, looking at the offending phone. Blake was the only one who had ever called him anything but his full name. Normally, he tolerated it, perhaps even liked it, because it reminded him of a happier time when his life with Donna was still very much ahead of him instead of part of the past.

But right now, being addressed as "Jeffy" irritated the hell out of him. "That's because I'm not looking, *Blakey,*" he shot back.

Emily decided that if they tag-teamed, she and Uncle Blake might be able to outmaneuver her father and wear him down until he surrendered. "Uncle Blake says that he's got tickets for the two of you—you and your date—to attend a performance art event." She tried to look confident, but inside she felt as if all her bones were crossing imaginary fingers.

"Performance art," Jefferson repeated as if it left a sour taste in his mouth. "Just what the hell is performance art?"

Emily waited a beat for her godfather to say something. When no sound emerged from the telephone, she quickly jumped in. "It's when—"

Jefferson waved his hand. Whatever it was, it sounded flaky and he had no patience with anything flaky. He was a rock-solid, button-down corporate lawyer who considered eating a steak with hot sauce daring. "Never mind. I don't need to know because I'm not going."

"Sylvie will be disappointed," Blake's loud, disembodied voice told him, purposely sounding mournful.

Jefferson frowned at the telephone. "I'm sure she'll get over it, whoever Sylvie is."

"Sylvie Marchand," Emily volunteered. Blake had given her a complete rundown before they'd joined forces to break the news to her father. She liked the woman already. She only prayed that when the time came, Sylvie Marchand would forgive her for fibbing on the application form. But that had been out of necessity. On paper, her father sounded deadly dull. Emily had a feeling no one would have been willing to go out with him. And he deserved the very best.

Which was what he was going to get if she had anything to say about it.

"She's your date, Dad."

He looked at his daughter and knew she meant well. But this was not something he was prepared to do for her. He wanted his life to remain uncomplicated, the way it had up until now. "She is *not* my date. I don't *want* a date."

Emily pressed her lips together and looked at him. A thought she'd never entertained before suddenly occurred to her and her eyes widened as it sank in.

"Dad, are you—you know…" Her voice trailed off as she found herself momentarily at a loss. But this was her father and she loved him. If she was going to do right by him, she needed all the facts. There was nothing to be gained by backing off. She just might need to revamp her plans. Taking a breath, she shot the question out. "Dad, do you like men?"

He looked at the receiver his daughter was holding and thought of the man on the other end. "Right now, only to go ten rounds with. And no, I am not 'you know,'" he informed her.

She offered him a sunny smile. The one he could so seldom resist. "Then why not go? Dad, this is a chance of a lifetime. You'll be sorry if you miss it." She paused. "How many reunions can you go to before people start dying?"

At sixteen, Emily thought everyone over the age of twenty-five was old. He knew that, but still, he had to admit he didn't exactly like the thought that his daughter was beginning to view him as having one foot in the grave.

There was a simple way to counteract that. He could act like a younger man.

Easier said than done.

Jefferson looked at her for a moment, then indicated the phone. "I don't like you two going behind my back this way."

"We wouldn't have to if you were more agreeable." Blake's voice rose in defense of their actions. "Emily and I only have your best interests at heart, Jeff. Right, Emily?"

"Right," she agreed heartily, then looked at her father. "Please, Dad? Please go to this reunion. Please see this lady that Uncle Blake found for you."

She blinked once, staring up at him with eyes that he could never resist, never truly say no to. When it came to Emily, he was a pushover.

With a sigh, Jefferson nodded. "All right, you win. I'll go."

He began to bend over to fish the invitation out of the garbage, where he had thrown it last night after tearing it in several pieces to ensure that it wouldn't reappear on his desk.

With a grin, Emily blocked his effort, pointing to the desk. When he moved toward it, he saw the invitation lying there again, taped together like a badly wounded war veteran. A war veteran now on the mend, with every hope of making a full recovery.

Picking the invitation up, Jefferson shook his head and then smiled. "I guess if you're this determined to see me go to this reunion, it's the least I can do."

Overjoyed, Emily threw her arms around his neck as Blake, overhearing, shouted, "Good man, Jefferson!"

CHAPTER TWO

AT THIRTY-FIVE, VIBRANT, redheaded Sylvie Marchand had an incredible zest for life. At one time a budding artist with considerable promise, she'd been around the block more than once. That block had led her to places like New York, Los Angeles and Paris, and along the way to several passionate, satisfying, relatively long-term relationships. The last of which, with a fading rock musician named Shane Alexander of the now defunct rock group Lynx, had actually been less satisfying than torrid and brief.

But it was this last relationship that had yielded her greatest treasure and joy in life: her three-year-old daughter, Daisy Rose.

Far from souring or jading her, the events of those earlier years had just made the third of Anne and Remy Marchand's four daughters aware that life had to be grabbed with both hands and, above all, savored. Those same events had also taught her what they'd taught Dorothy of Oz fame: there was no place like home. And family, if you were lucky enough to have one, should always come first.

Which explained why Sylvie now found herself

back in New Orleans after all this time. She had
returned home a year ago to run the art gallery that
was attached to her family's hotel, and she and her
oldest sister, Charlotte, who was now general
manager of the Hotel Marchand, had been here
when their mother, Anne, suffered a heart attack
four months ago.

The event had all but floored Sylvie, bringing the
glaring truth of mortality to her doorstep. Her beloved
father, Remy, had died all too young, in a tragic car
accident four years ago at the age of 61. That had
been difficult enough to weather, but Sylvie had never
thought that anything could happen to her mother.

Anne Robichaux Marchand had always been an
unstoppable force in Sylvie and her sisters' lives.
Years ago, Anne and Remy had been in the right
place at the right time and taken over a hotel whose
owner had fallen on hard times. The hotel, which
they'd renamed Hotel Marchand, was actually the
successful marriage of four town houses. With
Anne's guidance and Remy's culinary abilities, the
hotel became a four-star establishment. Tucked
away just east of Jackson Square in one of the
original blocks of the French Quarter, the hotel gave
welcome shelter to tourists who flocked to New
Orleans, especially during Mardi Gras season.

As far back as Sylvie could remember, her
mother had been a workaholic, a type-A personal-
ity whose batteries never seemed to need recharg-
ing. After her husband died, Anne only became more
driven, more dedicated to the hotel. The heart attack

had stopped her cold, but Anne insisted she needed to get back to work. There was a second mortgage on the hotel and Anne was afraid that business might drop off if she wasn't there to oversee everything.

Charlotte was convinced that the only way their mother could be persuaded to back off a little from her intense workload—and probably from working herself to death—was if she knew that her daughters were taking over the family business.

So Charlotte, who was already entrenched in every aspect of the hotel's inner workings, stepped in to their mother's position as general manager and sent out the call for Renee and Melanie, who had returned dutifully, if not completely eagerly, to the fold. Melanie brought her culinary skills into the kitchen of Chez Remy, the restaurant their father had made famous, while Renee, who had been a PR executive and producer at a mid-size studio in Hollywood, set about making sure the hotel retained its four-star rating.

As for Sylvie, well, her talents had always been in the arts. Not that many years ago, she had dreamed of becoming an artist herself. For a time, it had seemed she was on the right track. She'd been lucky enough to have a few minor shows of her work in a small gallery in New York, where she'd led a bohemian life and was willingly contemplating starving in some garret, preferably in Paris, for her craft. But her life had taken a different direction after a visit to Renee in Los Angeles. Sylvie had found work designing sets and had begun her short-lived affair with Shane. She'd still been living in L.A. when her mother had called and asked her if she would run the art gallery.

Sylvie had spent exactly a day debating whether to uproot her life again. She'd "talked" the decision over with a wide-eyed Daisy Rose at the playground, knowing full well that her little girl was going to say yes if it meant being close to her grandmother.

So, Sylvie had returned to New Orleans, the place that represented home in her dreams, and she had adjusted to her new, very respectable position. Running a gallery was not exactly the direction she had once seen her life going in. But it did allow her to stay very much involved with the art world and local artists, whose work she put on display in the two-story gallery.

Besides, she mused as she stood on the ground floor, just shy of the gallery's street entrance, overseeing the removal of several crates from a truck, the focus of her world had completely changed since she first left New Orleans. Then life had been all about her. She'd focused on her dreams, her path, her future. In Los Angeles, despite religiously practicing good birth control, she had become pregnant. And swiftly found herself abandoned.

After spending eight months lamenting her pending loss of freedom, she had found herself falling in love with the tiny baby she'd pushed out into the world after an excruciating fourteen hours of labor. With Daisy Rose in her arms, Sylvie had left the hospital knowing that she no longer had the luxury to be a reckless kid. Not when this perfect little being was depending on her.

So, she'd grown up. Sort of. But not completely. Her bohemian streak was still alive and well and thriving within her.

Her older sister Renee approached through the hotel entrance, waving a paper at Sylvie, and announced that it contained the profile of her prospective "date."

Sylvie stopped mid-gesture. She'd been about to signal the brawny, overweight trucker to put the crate against the wall. The gallery's parquet floors had just been buffed to high gloss and she wanted to make sure that neither of the two deliverymen tracked in any more dirt than necessary.

"Date?" she repeated, staring up at the strawberry blonde whose willowy figure she secretly envied. "What date?"

"Ms. March," the trucker mumbled into one of his two chins, abbreviating her surname as he struggled with the crate. It was obvious that he wanted to be back in the truck and on to his next destination.

"Put it over there." She gestured toward the wall farthest from the front entrance. "I just need you to take the tops off the crates and then you're done."

Her announcement was greeted with relief by both men. The truckers made her think of bulls in a china shop. There were several delicate sculptures displayed in the gallery, and the truckers were accidents looking to happen.

Renee shifted, blocking Sylvie's view of the

crates. "We thought that maybe it was time you had a little break in your life, Sylvie. You've been pretty driven these past few years."

Funny, Sylvie thought. *Driven* was the last word she would have used to describe herself. But then, so would *mother,* and here she was, enjoying that role most of all.

The taller of the two truckers brought her a clipboard with a crinkled yellow sheet to sign. She paused for a second to read it over and make sure she was signing for five paintings and not for the delivery of some East Indian elephant.

"We?" she asked, putting pen to paper and signing with a flourish. "Just who's 'we'?" She surrendered the clipboard and pen to the trucker, who tore off a copy for her and handed it back. "Certainly not Mother."

"No," Renee agreed, moving out of the way as the truckers ambled out the front entrance, pushing a huge dolly before them. "Not Mother. The rest of us. Charlotte, Melanie and me," she added for good measure.

For the first time, Sylvie glanced at the paper in Renee's hand. It was from a dating service. God, how very button-down. Had it come to that? she wondered. Did she need to be matched up with someone via a computer? It wasn't all that long ago she would just wander into a gathering of people, select someone she wanted to get to know and make eye contact. Nothing more was necessary. Now she'd been reduced to a collection of statistics input into a database.

The very thought sent chills zipping up and down her spine and made her want to grab her child and her paint box and flee.

Instead, she remained where she was, the irony of Renee's words bringing a hint of a smile to her lips. "So you think I need a little break. I find that kind of amusing, coming from the non-social three."

The street entrance door slammed shut, signaling the departure of the truckers. The three crates stood with their tops removed, waiting for their contents to be lifted out and displayed. Ordinarily, nothing would have kept Sylvie from it. The paintings inside had been sent over from a museum for a limited time. But for the moment, they took a back seat to what was unfolding before her.

A dating service?

What in heaven's name were her sisters thinking?

She shook her head, looking at Renee. "I don't exactly see the three of you kicking up your heels, either."

Renee stiffened ever so slightly. Love was something she had personally given up on. Most men she met wanted her solely as a decoration, arm candy to reinforce their own machismo. When they realized that there was an iron butterfly beneath the soft-spoken words, they quickly bowed out. She had become weary of having her hopes dashed and her heart used as a hockey puck. At thirty-seven, she'd never married and had come to the conclusion that she would remain that way.

But she had no children, and Sylvie did. It was

time for her younger sister to get busy and start looking for a father for Daisy Rose. "One pair of heels at a time, Sylvie."

Sylvie pressed her lips together to keep her smile from spreading. "Meaning you're next?"

Renee deliberately ignored the question. "I think this guy's a pretty good match for you." She pointed to one of the lines that listed interests. "Look, he likes the same kind of music you do. Hard rock." She pointed to another line. "And he says here that he likes taking chances." Renee glanced at the paper to make sure she got the wording right. "Thinks that life is a challenge—"

"It's a challenge, all right," Sylvie couldn't help murmuring under her breath.

Sometimes maybe too much of a challenge, she added silently. Growing up, she'd thought that the child had the hard part. Now she knew it was the parent who shouldered the worries and responsibilities. There were times when she wondered how much longer she would be able to go on doing this impossible balancing act. Life seemed to be filled with hundreds of tiny battles and even tinier victories.

For instance, last night she'd had the first decent sleep in over a week. Daisy Rose was just getting over a bad cold, one that seemed to kick into high gear like clockwork every night after midnight. Last night was the first time in eight days that the little girl had fallen back to sleep after waking up only once.

Tiny victories, she thought again.

"A *fun* challenge," Renee emphasized, bringing her back to the present.

Sylvie noticed that Renee had that smile on her lips, the one that used to drive her crazy when they were kids. Not quite superior and just a little smug, as if she was privy to something that younger sisters weren't allowed to know yet.

"You do remember fun, don't you, Sylvie?"

Sylvie made her way over to the first crate. These paintings weren't going to take themselves out. "Vaguely."

Renee followed her, shaking her head, her point driven home. "See, Sylvie, you're becoming stodgy."

Sylvie pretended to roll her eyes and placed the back of her hand to her forehead. "God forbid I turn into Charlotte."

"And just what's wrong with turning into me?"

Sylvie and Renee glanced around to see their older sister walking into the gallery through the hotel entrance. Anyone looking at the petite, slender woman with her exotic almond eyes and dark auburn hair would have guessed her to be closer to thirty than forty. All the Marchand women took after their mother and grandmother, both of whom looked to be ten to fifteen years younger than they were.

"I don't think I could be that much of a workaholic," Sylvie replied cheerfully, not missing a beat.

"It's an acquired taste," Charlotte replied dryly. "Besides, that's what this is all about." She tapped the piece of paper that was still in Renee's hand. "To keep you from becoming another me."

Charlotte had her own story. And her own heartbreak. In love with one man, she'd married another on the rebound. She'd tried her best to make a go of a less-than-perfect union, but the marriage was doomed from the start. Charlotte's husband turned out to have a penchant for romancing anything with a shapely pair of hips and evidently had no intention of giving up his hobby after marriage. Once they were divorced, Charlotte had thrown herself headlong into the family business, and hadn't come up for air since.

"If you ask me, you're the one who should be going out with—" Sylvie paused to read the name at the top of the application. "Mr. Jefferson Lambert." The line beneath it listed the applicant's occupation. "Look, he's a lawyer. That's perfect for you."

But Charlotte shook her head. "Not my type, Sylvie. Says right here he likes performance art, modern painters and hard rock music, which, to me, sounds like a male cat being neutered without benefit of anesthetic."

Sylvie crossed her arms before her, amused at the description. Charlotte might look young, but she had the tastes of someone from the previous generation. "You should learn to be more eclectic."

"I'll work on it in my spare time." This wasn't about her, Charlotte thought, it was about Sylvie. She really cared about Sylvie. They all did. And

Sylvie had practically been a nun since she'd moved back home, which was completely unnatural for her. According to Renee, she'd been pretty much like that ever since Daisy Rose was born. "So, are you game?"

A twinkle came into Sylvie's eye. "I'm always game, Charlotte."

Charlotte gave her a penetrating look. "Yes, that's how you got Daisy Rose. We all know that. I mean for this date."

Sylvie knew her sister was teasing—mostly. She'd been nothing but responsible ever since Daisy Rose had been a mere hint in her life. Still, maybe going out with this bought-and-paid-for match might be fun. Besides, it was only for one evening. What could it hurt?

"Maddy's giving one of her famous dinner parties," Renee interjected. "We thought that might be the perfect place for a first date."

"Or an 'only' one," Sylvie pointed out with a whimsical grin. "Maddy, huh?"

This had definite possibilities. Maddy O'Neill was as avant-garde as Sylvie had once been. The woman's newest performance events involved inviting a group of strangers to an informal dinner setting and letting them mingle. It made for some interesting conversations. So far, the events had been fairly successful and fun. Maddy's only requirement was that the groups be diverse, so she'd invited tourists and local citizens, highbrow and low.

Sylvie made up her mind. "Okay—why not? I'll

just brush the cinders out of my hair and leave the broom in the corner. What do I have to lose?" That put to rest, temporarily, she turned her attention to the crates that had been shipped to the gallery. "Okay, which of you lovely ladies is going to help me with these paintings?"

Renee raised her hands before her and backed away. "Sorry, just had my nails done."

Sylvie turned to her other sister. "Charlotte?" She pointed to an abstract on the wall. "I need to take that one down to make room for this new grouping."

"Sorry, Syl, I'm all thumbs. Call someone from Maintenance."

Sylvie sighed. "As if someone from maintenance would have any reverence for a Matthew Baldwin original." Baldwin was one of several local artists that Sylvie had agreed to promote.

Charlotte glanced over at the wall where the Baldwin was hanging. "They might have just the right perspective for a Matthew Baldwin original. It looks like what the kitchen tosses out at the end of the night."

"Peasant," Sylvie declared.

"I might be a peasant, but I know what I like," Charlotte replied cheerfully as she left the gallery.

JEFFERSON LOOKED AROUND the lobby of the Hotel Marchand as he walked toward the front desk. When he'd flown out of Boston this morning, the city was in the grip of the worst cold snap in fifty years. It had snowed for two days, stopping only yesterday morning.

New Orleans might as well have been a different world. Coming into the hotel, with its Southern Plantation decor, had transported him back in time, slipping him into a life he'd known more than two decades ago.

Not that he had ever specifically been here, at this hotel, but there had been other hotels, other clubs in the French Quarter. The ambiance, both outside the hotel walls and within them, brought back to him a part of his own past, a time when responsibilities did not sit so heavily on his shoulders and life offered much more freedom.

Although he'd always had a plan, a focus to his life, going to school in New Orleans had managed to pleasantly blunt the edges and make everything more relaxed. Even studying for exams. Life in New Orleans did not streak by on a lightning bolt the way it did back in Boston. Here people walked, they didn't run. They savored, rather than devoured. They lived life in the present, not the future, enjoying the moment.

He stopped to take a deep breath, then exhaled slowly. It was like being in a time warp. Even inside the hotel he could smell the sweet scent of honeysuckle and gardenias.

It seemed to go with the territory. The spacious lobby had warm gold-colored walls, hardwood floors and patterned burgundy, black and gold carpets. The sofas and chairs were a mix of neutral creams and reds, with just enough colorful tapestry pillows here and there to wake up the senses. The lobby was also filled with lush greenery and floral arrangements.

There was grace here, he thought. Grace, beauty and a sense of heritage that inspired awe and could only be admired and respected. Though he knew no one in the hotel, Jefferson felt a sense of homecoming. It pervaded everything. He was twenty-two again and the world was before him, full of promise and love.

He silently blessed Emily for being such a pushy kid and not giving up on him.

"Welcome to the Hotel Marchand," the man behind the front desk said the moment Jefferson drew close.

It was a phrase that the young clerk must repeat several hundred times each month, Jefferson thought, yet somehow he managed to make it sound fresh, warm. Personal. All part of the New Orleans charm, he mused. He was glad he'd come, glad he'd given in to Emily and Blake, who was meeting him later for a drink. Jefferson had resisted at the last moment, just before boarding the plane. There were contracts on his desk to go over and he wasn't thrilled about leaving Emily behind, even if it was in the capable hands of Sophie Beaulieu, his late wife's mother.

He supposed, if he thought about it, that there were a hundred reasons for him not to come, and only one real reason for him to be here. Because he needed to be.

Even though he would have hated to admit it out

loud, Blake and Emily were right. He needed a break from being Jefferson Lambert, full-time corporate lawyer, full-time dad and no-time man. Somehow, he'd lost himself in the shuffle. There had to be more to him than just work and fatherhood.

There had been, once. Being here was a chance to reconnect with the man Donna had fallen in love with.

"Your name, please?" the desk clerk asked brightly.

"Jefferson Lambert."

Keys began to click quickly as the young man typed in his name. "Is this business or pleasure?" he inquired with a wide smile as he hunted through the reservations for the name he'd been given.

"Pleasure." Jefferson had almost said "business" because business was the only thing that ever took him out of town, away from Emily. The last time he'd been away from home for reasons other than business had been on his honeymoon. A long time ago, he reflected.

The desk clerk frowned as he looked up from the computer screen. "I can't seem to find a reservation. Would it be under any other name?"

Jefferson shook his head. "No. Just mine."

Trying again, the clerk came up with the same results. He looked truly upset. "I am sorry, Mr. Lambert, but you don't seem to be listed here."

"Are you sure?" Jefferson curbed the urge to turn the computer around and do the searching himself. "The reservation was made over a week ago. My friend, Blake Randall, called it in for me."

"Blake Randall," the desk clerk repeated. More clicking as his fingers flew over the keyboard. "Maybe there was a misunderstanding and the reservation was placed under his name."

Without losing an iota of the wide, genial smile on his lips, the clerk flipped from one screen to another. After a few minutes, the smile began to fade.

"I'm sorry. It doesn't appear to be under Blake Randall, either."

There was no point in insisting that the reservation had to be there. Jefferson knew when to roll with the punches. "All right, maybe there was a mix-up. Just give me any room, then."

The desk clerk sighed. "I'm afraid that's impossible."

Jefferson stared at the man, puzzled. It seemed a reasonable enough request. "Why?"

The contrite expression on the clerk's face made his apologies for him, even though none of this was his fault. "Because this is the beginning of Mardi Gras season, sir. Everyone wants to be here this time of year. All of our rooms are booked."

Of course, Jefferson thought. But he was flexible. "Do you know where I can get a room?"

"Perhaps with a friend?" the clerk suggested tactfully, offering a weak smile.

Jefferson refused to believe that he'd come all this way, only to wind up standing in a lobby, albeit a beautiful one, with nowhere to go. He wasn't about to impose on Blake—that wasn't his style. Besides, he liked his privacy and Blake didn't know the meaning of the word.

"Do you mean to tell me there's no other room to be had in the city?"

The clerk tried again, quickly checking with the various hotels in the area. Because of Katrina, there weren't as many as there once had been. He frowned. "I'm afraid not, Mr. Lambert. The city is bursting at the seams. We're all celebrating our first full season since the hurricane almost did us in."

"Perhaps this wasn't such a good idea after all," Jefferson said, more to himself than to the man behind the desk. He'd never been one for omens, but this one was hard to ignore. The powers that be obviously thought it was a bad idea for him to resume dating, however briefly and inconsequentially, at his advanced age.

He had to face it. At forty-seven, he should be focused on funding his pension plan and making sure there was enough money to send Emily to the college of her dreams. And graduate school after that if she so desired. He had no business reentering the world of dating—a world he had never much cared for in the first place. Dating left you vulnerable. It stripped you down to your underwear and paraded you that way before the world at large. He'd survived it once and had had the incredible fortune of finding a beautiful woman to love him. That was more than enough for him.

"No, Mr. Lambert, it's never a bad idea to come

to New Orleans," the desk clerk told him quickly. "Let me try to make some calls—"

"Give him the Jackson Suite."

Jefferson turned toward the melodious voice behind him.

CHAPTER THREE

THE VOICE SOUNDED as if it belonged to a soft, genteel southern lady. One who might be given to spending long, languid afternoons in a lush, vine-covered garden, sipping something cool and refreshing beneath the shade of a gazebo while watching a willow weep in the gentle spring breeze.

That was not the woman he found himself looking at.

The woman who had suggested that the desk clerk place him in the Jackson Suite, whatever that was, looked very much like a model who had just stepped off the runway in Paris. And she was taking no prisoners.

Only conquests.

Her hair was an enthralling shade of red and fell in curls and waves about her oval face and shoulders like a storm churning at sea. The eyes that looked at him were almond shaped, green and extremely lively, yet not nearly as lively as her mouth, which had quirked into a smile that Jefferson was fairly certain could send strong men to their knees if she felt so inclined.

For reasons that Jefferson couldn't begin to fathom, she was looking at him as if she were studying him, trying to decide something. What, he didn't have a clue. But he knew that women who looked the way this one did, which was nothing short of drop-dead gorgeous, did not study men like him. Not with a mysterious gleam in their eye.

Oh, they might easily bring their financial woes to him, or ask for some kind of legal advice. But when any kind of active interest entered their gaze, their eyes were guaranteed to be focused in another direction and on someone else. Someone more ruggedly handsome. The only time he had attracted anyone remotely near this woman's league had been during his time as a tutor. Donna and he had attended Tulane together. She'd been in one of Blake's classes, which was how Jefferson came to meet her. His friend had suggested Donna seek him out because she had needed help in every subject but art, which was her passion.

And so, he'd become her tutor. At first for a fee, because that was how he'd earned money on the side back then. But it wasn't long before he was giving her help freely. As freely as he'd given, in secret, his heart.

Later, after they married and when he asked her how someone like him had gotten so lucky to win someone like her, Donna told him that luck had nothing to do with it. He had won her over with his gentle ways. It had taken a little over three years for him to go from tutor to boyfriend to husband. But even Donna had to admit that she hadn't thought of him "in that way" when she first met him. Or even within the first few months of their association.

So why was this woman looking at him as if she was trying to decide something about him, something very personal? Looking at him as if she could almost see everything about him clear down to the bone.

Careful, Jefferson, you're letting old memories get to you. Maybe it was the result of being back in New Orleans and its association with voodoo. In an uncharacteristic flight of imagination, he could easily picture this woman as a high priestess. Who was she, anyway?

That question was answered as the desk clerk cleared his throat and looked at the woman a bit subserviently.

"The Jackson Suite, Miss Sylvie? You sure? Miss Charlotte likes to keep that suite in reserve for unexpected guests." The reminder was tactful and the clerk seemed to be holding his breath, obviously hoping that he hadn't given offense.

'Miss' Sylvie's expression indicated that none was taken. If anything, she looked amused. "Well, I'd say that this guest appears to be quite 'unexpected.'"

She turned her vivid green eyes back to him. Jefferson found them unsettling—and completely fascinating. Very much, he realized, like the woman.

"Except that he himself expected to stay here and have a room waiting for him when he arrived." Her smile widened.

Jefferson felt something tighten in his stomach, like he was bracing himself before going down a steep incline in the first car of a roller coaster.

"Isn't that right, Mr. Lambert?"

Jefferson blinked, momentarily taken aback. He was about to ask her how she knew his name, then realized that she had overheard his exchange with the desk clerk.

"Yes," he murmured just as he became aware of something else. Pieces began to drift into place. Sort of. "He just called you Miss Sylvie."

"Yes. It's one of David's more charming habits," she said as she turned and smiled at the man behind the desk. David began to turn a shade of pink that, until this very moment, Jefferson hadn't thought was humanly possible. "'Miss' sounds ever so much nicer than being addressed as 'ma'am.' It gives the illusion of perpetual youth."

As if she needed an illusion, Jefferson thought.

"You wouldn't be Sylvie Marchand, would you?" he asked hesitantly.

Sylvie cocked her head, sending soft red hair cascading down her shoulder. "And why wouldn't I be?"

It had been a long time since Jefferson had felt youthful. Walking into the hotel had done it for a moment, but in reality, he and youth had parted company a long time ago. Looking at Sylvie Marchand, he suddenly felt older than ever. Granted, the woman wasn't exactly Emily's age, but she had to be around twenty years younger than he was.

Which meant, he suddenly realized, that he could have been Sylvie's father if he'd gotten started a great deal earlier in the procreation department than he actually had. Still, he held on to a little hope. After all, there could be more than one woman with that name. Maybe the young woman he was speaking to was his date's niece.

"You can't be Sylvie Marchand, because I am supposed to meet a Sylvie Marchand for a dinner engagement tomorrow evening."

A dinner engagement, Sylvie mused. How very formal sounding. She smiled at the man in front of the desk because it was second nature for her to put people at ease. A smile, she'd also learned, could effectively mask unsettling thoughts that might simultaneously be going on inside her head at the time. Like now. Thoughts that were coupled with questions.

Looks certainly could be deceiving. Jefferson Lambert seemed more like a professor from some small-town university than the dynamic criminal lawyer who handled high-profile cases that the application she'd been given said he was. And quite honestly, he looked as if he might enjoy spending an evening listening to a chamber ensemble play three-hundred-year-old music rather than dancing the night away to the beat of a hard rock band.

But he did look nice, she thought. Very nice. And he was tall. Probably about six-six. She'd always liked tall men. They made her feel more feminine and petite. And she liked his eyes. They were gray-blue, but more importantly, they were kind-look-ing. Right about now, she was fairly confident that she would take kind over sexy. Her last two lovers had had very sexy eyes. And, it turned out, very empty souls.

She continued to scrutinize the man, priding herself on being able to see people through an artist's eyes. Her prospective date looked as if he had a pretty good build, she decided. Of course, the clothes he was wearing didn't exactly highlight any portion of his physique, but there were no telltale bulges strategically covered, no buttons straining against an expanding waistline. And unless a tailor enhanced his jacket, the man had more than a decent set of shoulders. She was rather partial to broad shoulders.

"Maybe you're meeting her early," Sylvie sug-gested, a smile playing on her lips.

His eyes swept over her again. She was wearing what he thought Emily called a peasant blouse, and a skirt that seemed to come in two parts. A short, straight solid layer that covered a little more than the bare essentials and a much longer, wider, see-through layer of deep purples and royal blues. It was enough to make a man's pulse stop. This was a case of the whole being even greater than the sum of its parts—which from where he was standing were pretty damn good on their own.

"You're Sylvie Marchand." It wasn't a statement, it wasn't a question. It was an expression of shock.

Her eyes crinkled at the corners a little as she laughed. "Ever since I was born. Actually, it's Sylvia, but no one calls me that," she told him. "Sylvia is a little too conservative for me."

A faint, distant alarm went off somewhere in his head. Sylvie had wrinkled her nose ever so slightly when she'd said the word *conservative*. He wasn't sure if that was a signal of disdain. What he did know was that if there was one word that accurately described him, his life, his tastes, his goals, it would be *conservative*.

Training and manners, bred in him from the time he was toilet-trained, had Jefferson politely extending his hand to this vision.

"I'm Jefferson Lambert." And then he looked at her ruefully as she wrapped her fingers around his, returning the shake. The woman probably thought he was a dolt. "But then, I guess you've already figured that out."

Rather than render a sarcastic remark, Sylvie merely laughed. It was a sound reminiscent of wind chimes moving softly in a hot summer breeze. "I'm quick on the uptake that way, Jefferson."

"I just bet you are." And then he stopped, slightly stunned. He'd only meant to think those words, nothing more. "Did I just say that out loud?" He watched her face for some sign of offense and was relieved to see that there was none. On the contrary, she seemed sincerely amused by his bemusement. Perhaps by him.

Sylvie laughed as she withdrew her hand from his. He was kind of cute in a strange, funny sort of way. "Yes, and I kind of liked it."

"Um, Miss Sylvie, about the room," David began hesitantly.

Sylvie stopped him, instinctively knowing what the man was going to say. Life within the hotel might give the appearance of being as slow moving as molasses, but there were a great many type-A personalities working behind the scenes to perpetuate that illusion. Charlotte and her mother to name only two. But this issue was one that she was going to resolve in her own way.

"David, you have to learn to go with the flow. Now, unless my sister specifically instructed you to defend that empty suite with your last dying breath, between you and me, I think that it'll be all right to let Mr. Lambert make use of it for the duration of his stay in this fair city of ours." She looked at David pointedly. "Especially since someone on our staff must have lost his reservation."

David didn't look convinced. "Yes, ma'am, I mean Miss Sylvie."

Sylvie knew what was bothering him. Charlotte could be overbearing at times. And David was one of those people who lived in fear of a disapproving look.

"Don't worry," Sylvie assured him. "I'll explain it all to Charlotte. She won't say anything, since it was her idea to set me up with Mr. Lambert in the first place."

Caught off guard by the throwaway remark, Jefferson stared, dumbfounded, at the woman at his side. "Excuse me?"

Like some free-spirited gypsy holding court, Sylvie turned toward him, an expression he found unreadable, and at the same time irresistible, in her eyes. "I find honesty is always the best policy, don't you agree?"

He believed in honesty. It was his job not only to believe in it, but to uphold it. The firm he was with had a spotless reputation and had welcomed him into the fold, after a lengthy investigation, like a long-lost brother. He'd long ago vowed never to let his firm, himself or Emily down. Not even little white lies could be attributed to him.

"Yes. Of course. But I don't see what that has to do with—"

She second-guessed where he was going with his question and headed him off. "My sisters Charlotte, Melanie and Renee thought I was working too hard and needed a little fun in my life."

Because Emily and Blake had gone behind his back and filled out an application for a matchmaker on his behalf, Jefferson made the connection. Although, in Sylvie's case, he didn't understand why there wasn't a whole flock of men standing in the hallway, waiting for the slightest indication that she was interested.

"And I'm it?" he asked incredulously.

Sylvie had to bite her tongue to keep from laughing out loud. He did have the sweetest look of surprise and disbelief on his face. He was flattering her without really uttering a word. And he seemed to be modest. How unique.

"Apparently."

Jefferson thought about Sylvie's application, which Emily had given him to read. It seemed to have been written about another woman, a more *conservative* woman, for lack of a better word. Definitely not the vision in purples and blues before him. Maybe it would be better all around if he stopped this before it became too embarrassing. For both of them.

"You know," he began slowly, "I think there's been some mistake."

Aware that David's ears seemed to be growing as he leaned, none too subtly, over the desk, Sylvie drew Jefferson aside. "Why?"

He'd half expected her to cheerfully declare "Okay," and walk away. It was something a gypsy would have done, he was sure. But because she asked, he did his best to explain. "Well, to begin with, your age."

She didn't follow him. "What about my age?"

As if she didn't know, he thought. "The form said you were thirty-four."

She opened her mouth, about to say that she was, but remembered her remark about honesty. She had to tell him the truth. "That's wrong."

Well, at least she didn't think he was born yesterday, Jefferson thought. "Yes, I know."

"I'm thirty-five." Renee must have been the one to doctor that, Sylvie figured. Renee thought it was a sin for a woman to admit to being over thirty. Sylvie was surprised her sister hadn't made her twenty-nine.

Jefferson could only stare at Sylvie in disbelief. Most women did not delight in saying they were older than they were. "What?"

"Thirty-five," she repeated slowly, her lips caressing each syllable. "That's the number that comes after thirty-three *and* unfortunately, thirty-four."

He ignored the humor in her eyes, although it wasn't easy. "That's not possible."

The man really was a dear, Sylvie thought. He sounded as if he truly meant what he was saying. "I've got a birth certificate to prove it," she volunteered, amusement curving her lips.

His eyes narrowed. "You look like you're twenty-five."

Compliments, genuine compliments, were something a girl never tired of hearing, she decided. And his had a ring of sincerity. She wondered if that was a skill he'd acquired as a lawyer.

"The form didn't mention that you had a silver tongue, Jefferson."

She made his name sound like a melody, Jefferson thought. "No, but I do have twenty-twenty vision," he countered. He didn't add that the numbers had been recaptured only after he'd had the eye surgery he'd been putting off for so long. It wasn't vanity that had prompted him, but rather a desire to be free of the headaches that wearing glasses for half his life had caused him.

Sylvie was silent for a moment as she reassessed the situation. And the man. At first glance, he seemed stuffy, but that could have been because he was uncomfortable about this blind-date situation. Not everyone could move as freely as she could from person to person, situation to situation. And even she was beginning to find herself less flexible that way.

Maybe it was a sign of pending maturity, but she'd begun to question the purpose of her life even before she'd become pregnant with Daisy Rose. She knew she was a more subdued version of herself these days. She had a feeling that Jefferson Lambert might find that difficult to believe.

Sylvie glanced at the suitcase on the floor beside him. It couldn't contain all that much, no matter how great a packer the man was. "Is that the only luggage you brought with you?"

Jefferson felt he'd packed everything he needed. He was a man who knew how to make do. "I don't like having to stand around at the airport, waiting to see if someone finally decided that my suitcase should be sent down the luggage chute rather than on a separate trip to another state without me."

He watched her mouth turn up in response to his words. It was like watching the sun rise, casting golden rays in all directions.

He felt caught up in a sunbeam.

"I like traveling light, too," she told him as she slipped her arm through his. Turning to the desk clerk, she put her hand out. "Can I have the key card for the Jackson Suite, David?"

Aside from long, shapely legs, a neat trick for a petite woman, Sylvie Marchand also had long fingers, Jefferson noted. He wondered if she played any kind of instrument. Fingers like that looked as if they could glide effortlessly along a keyboard.

Or a man's skin.

The thought came out of nowhere. Banking it down, Jefferson attributed it to the fact he was in New Orleans. Thoughts like that belonged to a much younger man, a man who had the world before him.

"I'll need you to sign in and also give me a credit card for an imprint," David replied.

"Oh, sorry," Jefferson murmured. The woman had gotten him completely disoriented, he thought, handing the clerk a credit card. The young man swiped it as Jefferson registered.

The desk clerk handed back the credit card, along with a key card to the room. As he accepted both, Jefferson found himself on the receiving end of a brilliant smile from Sylvie Marchand. He felt his knees weakening just a tad.

"C'mon." She tugged gently on his arm. "I'll show you to your room."

"Um, how should I bill this, Miss Sylvie?" David called as they started to leave.

"The same as our regular rooms, David," she tossed capriciously over her shoulder. "Our mistake, remember? Can't have people saying we turn out our guests now, can we?"

"No, Miss Sylvie," David murmured, retreating.

"Your eyes twinkle," Jefferson observed as they made their way through the crowded lobby. There was a grand spiral staircase just past the front desk, but Sylvie kept walking. "I didn't think eyes could really do that."

"This is New Orleans, Jefferson," she drawled. "Everything is possible." And then she winked. "Especially around Mardi Gras season."

The doors to the elevator were just beginning to close when they reached it. Instead of standing back, the way he'd expected, she surprised him by pulling him along in her wake and wedging herself into the small space that was still available in the crowded car. He found himself standing almost closer to her than her clothes.

Sylvie rose on her toes, her body brushing against his. "You can breathe, Jefferson," she whispered in his ear. "It's okay."

So he breathed. And felt every inch of her against him.

He figured this was what dying and going to heaven had to be like.

When the doors opened on the third floor, Sylvie shouldered her way out, her hand still wrapped around his. He had no choice but to follow, apologizing to the man whose knees he hit with his suitcase.

"Voila," she announced after swiping the key card and opening the door. Sylvie stood back, allowing him to enter the suite first.

If he traveled at all, which was infrequently, Jefferson was accustomed to small, functional rooms that usually came with tiny kitchens. Away from home, he liked to cook his own meals, avoiding the expense and noise of restaurants and the discomfort of eating alone while everyone around him had someone to carry on a conversation with. He was not prepared for the grandeur that met his eyes.

The room was huge. There were paintings, originals, on two of the walls, depicting an antebellum New Orleans. And on either side of the king-size, canopy bed was a window that afforded him a view of the courtyard.

He crossed to the window on the left and looked out, thinking of the snowy scene he'd left back home just hours ago. A feeling of peace and seclusion pervaded the entire area. The sun grazed the top of the pool, shimmering invitingly. He forgot that it was January.

The view was mesmerizing, and in a way, he was sorry that Emily couldn't be here with him to enjoy it.

"Do you like it?" Sylvie asked.

"Like it?" he echoed incredulously. He glanced at her over his shoulder. "I don't know what to say."

She laughed, thinking of their date tomorrow evening. "Then bring flash cards."

Her speech might be slow, he thought, but her mind was quick. It obviously jumped around from topic to topic, losing him in the process. "Excuse me?"

"To our dinner party tomorrow night," she reminded him. "It's at seven. I'll meet you in the lobby at six-thirty."

He found himself nodding like some idiot who had been struck dumb. Finding his tongue, he asked, "Do you live in the hotel?"

"No." She still cherished her independence, such as it was. "I live a few miles away, but I'll meet you here," she repeated.

Now, there was another indication that she wasn't quite as care free as she'd once been, Sylvie thought. Not all that long ago, she'd have had no qualms about telling a man where she lived. But again, that was before she had Daisy Rose. She didn't want her little girl's life disturbed by anyone.

Even gentlemen callers, she thought, amused.

Sylvie glanced toward the old-fashioned clock on the mantel. It was getting late. She'd promised Maddy she would come by to help her set up for tomorrow. Sylvie moved toward the door.

"Until tomorrow night, then."

Her words floated softly to him. And then she was gone.

Jefferson stood there for a moment, just staring at the closed door wondering if he had imagined the whole thing, including Sylvie Marchand. *Especially* Sylvie Marchand.

But then he shook his head. No, the woman was real. He hadn't imagined her. His imagination had never been that creative.

Turning from the door, he went to phone Blake to let him know that he had arrived. Maybe in more ways than one.

CHAPTER FOUR

JEFFERSON NODDED his thanks to the bartender—
Leo, according to the name tag pinned to his navy
blue vest—as the man placed the chunky glass of
scotch and soda before him. The man's face showed
more than a little mileage, even in this light. He
nodded and withdrew.

Blake and Jefferson had gotten the last two empty
stools at the bar. Tucked away in the far corner of
the hotel across from the retail shops, the dimly lit
bar was doing brisk business tonight. Tomorrow was
the Twelfth Night celebration, the official beginning
of the Mardi Gras season, and tourists and natives
alike were starting the partying early.

Soft blue lights played off the surface of his drink,
and Jefferson raised the glass to his lips and took a
healthy swallow. He could feel the bitter liquid burn
its way through his chest down into his stomach.
Only then did he turn toward Blake and say what had
been burning with equal fervor in his brain.

"She's too young for me."

Sighing, Blake shook his head. The reason he'd
pushed so hard to get Jefferson to come down here

for the reunion in the first place was to counteract this delusion of advancing age his friend seemed to be suffering. Forty-seven was the new thirty-seven, and the last time Blake had looked, thirty-seven was not considered old in anything but dog years.

He swirled the ice cubes in his glass, listening to them clink against one another. Tipping the glass back, he took a long swallow of the Southern Comfort he'd ordered.

"Jeffy, I've already said this more than once. It's all in the mind." To emphasize his point, he brushed his index finger against Jefferson's temple. "The way you're acting, Mother Teresa would be too young for you."

Jefferson raised his eyes to Blake's. "Mother Teresa's dead."

"My point exactly." But that point, he could see, was not piercing the haze around his friend's brain. He leaned in to Jefferson. Because of the din in the crowded room, he brought his lips close to his friend's ear. "We only go around once in life, Jeff. You've got to loosen up, make the most of it."

Resting his drink on the bar, Jefferson placed both hands around it, as if surrounding a thought and trying to contain it. "I already went around once in life, Blake. I got my law degree, married a beautiful woman and had a wonderful daughter with her." His mouth curved as fond memories rushed back to him. Memories of Donna and falling in love for the first time. The only time. "The way I look at it, I'm way ahead of the average man."

He didn't mean to look at Blake when he said that, but there it was. Blake might be the one whose social book was bursting at the seams, with a different woman coming into play each month or so, like the changing faces of pinups on a calendar, but he'd had the richer life, Jefferson thought. He was the one who had experienced real love.

And, most importantly, he'd had a family. Blake had only ticket stubs from the various trips he'd gone on, the various clubs he'd visited, the various functions he'd attended. Things like that might have eaten up Blake's time, but they didn't create the kind of memories that Jefferson would have wanted for himself.

"You're only forty-seven years old, for crying out loud, not a hundred and forty-seven." For a moment, Blake's attention seemed to be drawn away by the smile of a blonde, two stools over, who was wearing a very fitting, very small black dress, but then he brought his focus back to Jefferson. "It's not time to lie down in the coffin yet."

Jefferson noted the way Blake was eyeing the blonde. Trying to meet and strike up a conversation with a stranger held absolutely no appeal for him. "You act as if I don't do anything but sit in a corner and stare at the walls. Most days, I've barely got two minutes to rub together."

Blake made a disparaging sound as he dismissed Jefferson's objection. "That's work."

"That's purpose," Jefferson countered. Besides, he liked his work. It was useful and necessary.

Industry would grind to a halt without corporate lawyers. The business world would dissolve in a sea of squabbles and heated arguments over rights and infringements.

Blake spread his hands, not in surrender but as if widening the playing field. "All I'm saying is, have a little fun before you can't. You're still a decent looking guy—"

Jefferson laughed, taking another sip of his drink. "Thanks."

"Hey, we all can't be studs like me."

Jefferson had a feeling that Blake was speaking only half tongue in cheek. It didn't bother him. When they were younger, it was Blake who had always attracted the girls. But then, Jefferson had been the one who'd gotten the only girl who counted.

"The point is," Blake continued, "you came down here, we're going to have a fantastic time at the reunion, and you're going to have a terrific date tomorrow night with Sylvie." He paused, as if preparing to drop a bombshell. "Her family owns this hotel, you know."

As if that would make a difference to Jefferson. When he married Donna, he'd also taken on her school loan. Wealth, or lack of it, had never mattered to him.

Jefferson smiled, amused. "So now you're turning me into a gigolo?"

Instead of denying it, Blake laughed. "Hey, it's as easy to love a rich woman as a poor one."

Jefferson's chunky glass met the top of the bar abruptly. He stared at Blake in disbelief. Just what was it that his friend and daughter were plotting? "Love? Who said anything about love? Aren't you getting way ahead of yourself here?"

Again, there were no denials, no backpedaling. The look on Blake's face was enigmatic. "Just leave yourself open to the possibilities, Jeff. Sylvie sounds like she could really open up your eyes—not to mention your pores."

Pores. As in the old wives' tale that having sex cleared up your skin. That was definitely a lot more than he had signed on for. "My pores are just fine, Blake."

"Oh?" Blake made no secret of scrutinizing his friend's complexion as he asked, "When was the last time you were with a woman?"

Jefferson was aware that Leo was back in their area. The taciturn man appeared to be listening as he prepared two mai-tais, even though he never raised his eyes from the blender.

"I'm with women all the time," Jefferson replied matter-of-factly.

But Blake shook his head. "I'm talking one-on-one, Jeff."

"You're talking too much," Jefferson retorted. He made an impulsive decision. No, it was the right decision, he amended. Saying yes in the first place had been impulsive. "Look, I think I'm going to cancel. You and I can spend tomorrow night catching up, instead," he suggested, then grinned. "I figure the way you live, that should take about a week."

Blake was having none of it. He wasn't about to let his friend bail out. "I've always hated one-sided conversations. Besides, didn't I tell you? I'm going to be busy tomorrow night."

This was the first Jefferson had heard of it. Blake had promised to be available every day of his stay in New Orleans. That was part of the deal. "Oh?"

"Yeah, attending that performance art function at the gallery in the Warehouse District."

"The one I'm attending," Jefferson said, purely for clarification.

"Yes. I know the woman who's running it. As a matter of fact—" his grin nearly split his dark, handsome face "—I'm dating the woman who's running it."

Jefferson could only shake his head. He had long since lost track of the number of women that Blake had dated. "Why doesn't that surprise me?"

Blake pretended not to hear. "And, as it turns out, Sylvie Marchand is one of her closest friends. So you see, Jefferson, you *have* to go or I'm going to have a miserable time."

Jefferson set his empty glass on the counter. Leo materialized, seemingly out of nowhere, a fresh drink in his hand. It was a carbon copy of the last one, right down to the number of ice cubes. About to decline, Jefferson changed his mind and nodded. Leo slid the drink on to a napkin and ushered it into the space the first drink had occupied.

"Miss Sylvie's good people," he told Jefferson. "Treat her right." The words almost sounded like a warning. The next moment, he'd moved to another part of the bar.

Slightly unnerved, Jefferson looked at Blake, trying to pick up the thread of their conversation before the bartender had made his comment. "I don't see the connection."

Blake obligingly spelled it out for him. "Maddy's not going to be happy if her friend gets stood up. Especially since I was the one who made the arrangements in the first place."

"You?" Jefferson's dark eyebrows drew together in a disapproving line. "You set me up with that kid? Did you get a look at her before you did this?"

"She's not a kid, she's a woman. Gotta watch those terms, lawyer man." Blake pretended to look around him. Jefferson noted that he made eye contact again with the blonde in the abbreviated black dress. "Around here, that kind of talk can get you castrated. Fast. Anyway, when Emily said she wanted to send in your application to an online dating service, I told her to hold on to her money. That I knew someone who did that sort of thing for a living. I persuaded her—"

"Her?"

"My friend who owns the matchmaking service, Gloria Conway," Blake clarified. Jefferson was trying to get all his facts straight. Blake could only smile. You could take the man out of the law firm, but you couldn't get the law firm out of the man.

"Anyway, I persuaded Gloria to let me take a look at the applications she had—"

But Jefferson wasn't finished with that part of it yet. "Isn't that unethical?"

A lawyer himself, Blake had never been the stickler for ethics that Jefferson was. The way he saw it, the two of them provided the yin and the yang of every situation, and balance was the key. "All's fair in love and war, Jeffy, you know that."

No, Jefferson thought, there was nothing fair about love or war. And tomorrow night, he was determined, was going to be neither. But this discussion they were having could go on all evening. He might consider himself the more able lawyer, but Blake was the pit bull when it came to winning. He'd been that way on the tennis court and in any kind of competition.

Taking a long sip of his drink, which was no longer fiery but oddly soothing, Jefferson surrendered. "Okay, I'm not going to have any peace until I go along with this."

Victory always made Blake magnanimous. "You're not going to regret it, Jeffy."

He didn't know about that, Jefferson thought. An uneasy feeling at the back of his neck told him he was walking into uncharted territory, a terrain with hidden sinkholes scattered throughout.

One wrong step and he would be in way over his head.

MADDY O'NEILL PUT DOWN the end of the table that she was carrying and pushed a strand of short, black hair out of her eyes. She stared at the woman on the other end of the table. "You met him?"

"By accident. He was checking in, I was on my way out. The front desk lost his reservation." Sylvie shrugged, sending the shoulder of her blouse sliding down. "So I had David give him the Jackson Suite." She looked at Maddy intently. "Are you going to carry your end, or is the table just going to levitate into place?"

With a sniff, Maddy picked up the table and resumed walking backward in small, measured steps. "You gave him the Jackson Suite?" she marveled. "You mean that delicious room that's supposedly an exact replica of the one Andrew Jackson shared with his wife before she died?" Deciding that this was as good a place as any to set down the first of three long dining tables, she lowered her end again. "Okay," she instructed with a nod.

Sylvie was all too happy to comply. "What do you mean, supposedly? I went through a lot of trouble to research that. It *is* an exact replica. Except for the paintings, of course. Those are mine."

Maddy crossed to the rear exit to retrieve the next table. "Yours? As in from the hotel gallery?"

"As in from my own brush," Sylvie corrected. When Maddy looked at her, she added, "I offered to help update some of the rooms—on a very limited budget—and wanted to add a personal touch." Bracing herself, she picked up the end of the second table and they began walking back into the gallery. "I'm very proud of that room."

"It's a gorgeous room." Maddy glanced over her shoulder to make sure she wasn't going to bump into the first table. "You've got a lot of talent, Sylvie, although I never pegged you for the research type." Reaching their destination, she put down her end. "But then, I never pegged you for the mother type, either, and you seem to be doing a beautiful job in that department."

Nothing made Sylvie prouder. Or happier. The satisfaction that came with being a mother had been a total surprise to her, like discovering one last, hidden present beneath the Christmas tree after all the torn wrapping paper had been cleared away.

"In a way, I think we're raising each other," she told Maddy. "Daisy Rose is raising me as much as I'm raising her." Her thoughts drifted from the room, sifting through the wealth of memory fragments that made up her life with Daisy Rose.

They crossed the room together to bring in the last of the tables. "Ever hear from that loser father of hers?"

"No, and I'm grateful for that." It was a lie. Sylvie had heard from him, or would have if she'd answered the phone. Shane had called her twice in the past two weeks, leaving messages that he wanted to talk to her. Out of the blue, after all this time. Well, he might want to talk to her, but she didn't want to talk to him. Ever.

The two women worked silently until the final table was in place.

"Having Shane in Daisy Rose's life would mean

nothing but trouble," Sylvie said, frowning. "He'd probably hit her up for cash if he could."

"Never knew what you saw in him."

Maddy could be counted on for brutal honesty, and this time she was right. "From this vantage point, I'd have to agree with you. I guess you just had to be there." She thought of the first time she'd seen the lead guitarist for Lynx. He'd blown her away. Shane Alexander seemed to become one with his instrument, with the music. "He was pretty hot stuff when he and the band were at the top." Her smile was rueful. "I got him just as he was on his way down. He needed reaffirmation and I needed to be needed, I suppose."

Maddy brought out one of the tablecloths she intended to use tomorrow night. Sylvie took an end, and together, they brought the cloth down over the table like a giant scarlet parachute descending to earth.

"He was one hell of a good time in bed. Unfortunately, out of bed he was pretty useless." She didn't like to think of herself as naive, especially at that point in her life, but she'd actually believed, for a very short time, that Shane loved her. She had had a rude awakening. "And then when I realized he had an intimate relationship with every single bottle in Southern California, not to mention every female over the age of eighteen, I split. He brought new meaning to the words *shallow* and *narcissistic*."

Maddy was all sympathy. "Hasn't he tried to get in contact with you?"

Biting her tongue to hold back the urge to share, Sylvie shook her head. "Not even once." Which, she told herself, would have been the truth had Maddy asked the question two weeks ago. "I sent him a card, care of the band, to let him know when Daisy Rose was born, and another on her first birthday, but he never acknowledged receiving either."

"Did he even know he was the father?" Maddy asked.

Sylvie laughed shortly. "Oh, he knew all right. His exact words at the time were 'Get rid of it.'" She tossed her head, summarily dismissing all thought of the man. "As far as I'm concerned, Daisy Rose might as well have had a test tube for a father. It probably would have been better that way for her, when you come right down to it."

"Oh, I don't know. Some good came of her having Shane as a father," Maddy theorized as she took out the second tablecloth. "For a little thing, she's got a very pretty voice."

Sylvie beamed with pride. Daisy Rose loved to sing to her dolls. "Certainly didn't get the ability to carry a tune from me. Hopefully, though, she'll be artistic."

Maddy was a firm believer in people making their own choices in life. Her parents never would have foreseen her becoming an artist. "Don't go making plans for her just yet. She might surprise you and be some kind of scientific genius."

Once they'd covered the third table, Sylvie began to bring over the folding chairs. "I don't want a genius, just a happy kid. That's part of the reason I came back, so that she could grow up with her family around her." She supposed she sounded overly sentimental, but there was nothing wrong with that. Sentiment had an important place in her world. "I grew up with a hell of a supportive family. I want Daisy Rose to experience that support, too. It fosters a sense of well-being."

"She might get that from having a father," Maddy tactfully pointed out as she dragged over the first of many chairs.

"Maybe. But I'm not about to put out an all-points bulletin looking for one," Sylvie assured her.

Leaving Maddy to handle the chairs, she went to the crate she'd brought with her. Inside were two paintings from the Hotel Marchand gallery, both by Louisiana artists—her contribution to tomorrow night's event. She'd brought them over personally to assure their safety, and she knew Maddy had hired extra security.

"I won't say that I'm not open to the idea," she continued. She was always open to life. "But if it doesn't happen, it doesn't happen. I don't need a man to complete me."

Maddy slid a chair beneath the table. "You're a better man than I, Gunga Din."

Sylvie gave her an incredulous look. "You? You're one of the most 'complete' women I know."

Maddy grinned. "Maybe so, but nothing beats a warm body next to yours when you slip into bed."

"I've had my share of warm bodies. The concept is highly overrated."

Bringing over two more chairs, Maddy stopped to look at her quizzically. "Then why are you going out with this guy tomorrow?"

One by one, Sylvie carefully leaned the paintings against the wall where she thought they should be hung. "Because I'm flexible. Because Charlotte, Melanie and Renee will get on my case if I back out. And because, after seeing him, I think he's kind of cute, although he's definitely not what I envisioned. I thought I was getting Johnny Depp and this guy's more like Gregory Peck. Now, I've always liked Gregory Peck," she qualified, "but Johnny Depp really gets my pulse going."

Instead of opening up the next two chairs, Maddy just leaned them against the table. "Did you ever see *Duel in the Sun?* Gregory can be a real bad boy, too."

"I'm not out for a bad boy," Sylvie interjected, then added, "I don't really know what I'm out for. But Jefferson Lambert is definitely not my type."

"What do you mean? According to his application, you and Jefferson have a lot of things in common."

"When did you see his application?" Was it posted in the town square? Or had Charlotte just run off copies for the world at large?

"Blake showed it to me."

"Blake?" She wasn't familiar with the name. Maddy went through men like a person with allergies went through tissues during hay fever season.

"My newest honey," Maddy explained. "Tall, dark, handsome. Rich, I think." Her eyes fairly gleamed as she went over his good points. "He's coming here tomorrow night. As it happens, he's friends with your guy."

Sylvie stiffened slightly. That sounded much too personal. Much too confining. "I don't have a 'guy.'"

"Okay, your temp," Maddy corrected with a laugh. "Anyway, Blake and Jefferson go way back. They both went to school here. Tulane," she added. "They were fraternity brothers. That's what Jefferson is doing down here in the first place. There's this big fraternity reunion taking place this week."

Somehow, Sylvie couldn't quite picture the man she'd met earlier being hazed and washing a walkway with a toothbrush. He had too much dignity for that.

But then, she reminded herself, she had no way of knowing what he'd been like as a college student.

"Nothing like a bunch of grown men trying to recapture their childhood," she commented. She saw the thoughtful look that came over Maddy's face. "What?"

"Nothing." Very slowly, Maddy surveyed the gallery space that she'd chosen for tomorrow's event. "You just might have given me an idea for another one of these gatherings."

Sylvie reviewed her last couple of sentences, then gave up. "I'm not even going to ask." She took out the hammer and nails she'd brought with her. "Sometimes, Maddy, you're even too off the wall for me."

"I'll take that as a compliment." Staring at the far

wall, Maddy fisted her hands at her waist and tried to envision it in a different color. "Think it's too late to paint that bright orange?"

"Much too late," Sylvie assured her. At the very least, orange would have clashed with one of the paintings she'd brought. "But if you're really going for a different look, we could have wall treatments." She was thinking out loud, the intensity in her voice rising as the idea gelled. "I know this place that would be willing to lend us coverings that look like textured wallpaper." She could already see them in her mind. "Might make a difference in the look of the place."

Maddy gave her a quick embrace. "I don't know what I'd do without you."

Sylvie laughed. "I thought that was why we were friends."

For a single moment, Maddy became serious. "We're friends because you're the best, the kindest and most generous person I've ever known."

Picking up her hammer, Sylvie got back to the business of hanging the paintings. "You're only saying that because it's true."

Maddy watched for a moment, then went to bring over more chairs. "If one of us was a man, this might lead somewhere."

"If one of us was a man, we wouldn't have been friends this long." Once she'd hammered in the nail, Sylvie hung up the first painting. She moved back to gain perspective and make sure the painting was straight. "Men have their place, but it's generally not in a woman's life."

"Boy, I can't wait for tomorrow night. You and your date might just wind up the focal point of our evening."

About to hammer in the second nail, Sylvie stopped dead. She knew how Maddy's mind worked. Her friend would think nothing of turning the spotlight on her. "Don't you dare," Sylvie warned.

"You turning shy on me, Syl?" Not that she would believe it for a minute.

"No." The word was reinforced with several measured raps of the hammer. "But I have a feeling Jefferson might be."

"Protective already," Maddy mused. "I think this bodes well."

"Not protective," Sylvie corrected. She did *not* want this getting out of hand, and if she let Maddy make assumptions there were sure to be tabloid stories the morning after the event about the lawyer and the "hotel heiress." "I just don't want the evening blowing up in my face, that's all. Or drawing itself out," she tacked on, because the latter would probably be more accurate.

"What are you wearing?"

Sylvie shrugged carelessly, concentrating on the second and larger painting. "I haven't decided yet."

Amused, Maddy could only shake her head. "You're the only woman I know who doesn't agonize over clothes. Of course, if I had your figure, I'd look good wearing a cereal box."

Sylvie laughed. "Now I remember why we're

friends. Because you're blindly loyal." Finished, she put down her hammer and hung up the painting. Perfect. "I'm going to call that woman about the wall treatments." She took out her cell phone.

Being busy kept her mind off the following evening—and the nerves that were suddenly and unaccountably mutinying in her stomach.

CHAPTER FIVE

IT WAS BECAUSE SHE'D BEEN out of the loop for so long, Sylvie decided the next evening. There was no other explanation for the strange, almost uncertain feeling she was experiencing.

She sat in the back of the cab she was taking from her apartment to the hotel, watching as the driver maneuvered through narrow streets that barely seemed to have room for people, much less cars. The distance was just a few miles, and the driver was keeping up a steady stream of conversation, but his words amounted to only so much noise buzzing about the outer edges of her thoughts. Her mind was otherwise occupied.

On her way to meet Jefferson Lambert, she was sailing out with less than her usual confidence. So much so that she'd had second thoughts. Which was completely unlike her.

Going out had always equaled having fun. She'd never been the kind to have her heart flutter, her hands grow damp or her feet feel as if they were literally getting cold. Yes, she'd felt weak in the knees a time or two, but that had been the fun part. She used to like diving into a new adventure, a new relationship. A new man.

Now, for some reason, there was this uneasiness in the pit of her stomach.

Life as Daisy Rose's mother had subdued her more than she'd realized.

Someone set off a row of fireworks and the noise brought her around for a second. She leaned forward to see, but they were driving through the crowded French Quarter now, and the darkness that had descended made it difficult to make things out. Sylvie leaned back again, lost in her thoughts. The driver continued talking. Something about people not knowing how to handle fireworks.

She still had a desire to embrace every day. But now her focus was on arranging a new sale for the gallery, or closing up shop early to get in an extra hour with her daughter.

There was a time, not all that long ago, when "possibilities" meant catching a flight to Paris on someone's private jet, or running off to Acapulco for the day. Or the week. Whatever the spirit moved her to do at the moment. Back then, she was up for everything and there was no such thing as tomorrow. Having Daisy Rose in her life made her very conscious of tomorrow. And all the tomorrows that were to come.

So, Sylvie concluded with a suppressed, impatient sigh, having turned into this semi-conservative person might be what was responsible for her feeling a little less than a hundred percent secure about the evening that lay ahead of her.

She shifted in her seat, careful not to wrinkle her dress. The one thing she was confident about was the way she looked tonight. She had a passion for clothes, and combining it with her love of art, she took more than a little pleasure in putting together outfits for both herself and Daisy Rose.

Tonight she was wearing a gently clinging silk dress with soft ruffles around the rather low cut neckline and scalloped hem. She'd silk-screened the lime-green and pink fabric herself. To offset the romantic impression that the dress created, she'd overprinted a veve, a ritual symbol inspired by New Orleans' voodoo tradition. It had eight sides and looked like a hot-pink starburst with blue edges.

As a finishing touch, she'd piled her riotous red hair on top of her head, securing it with a few strategically placed pins.

"You look pretty, Mama," Daisy Rose had proclaimed when she saw Sylvie emerge from her bedroom less than half an hour ago.

Sylvie had laughed. Nothing else mattered, she'd thought, but the way she looked in her little girl's eyes. She'd kissed the top of Daisy Rose's head. "Thank you, pumpkin."

"Well, there's no arguing with that," Anne Marchand had said with an approving nod as she looked her daughter over. "You are a vision."

"An apparition is more like it. When are you going to put some meat on your bones, girl?" Celeste Robichaux spoke up from the deep maroon winged armchair that she favored. It went with nothing else in the living room, but Sylvie had placed it there out of deference to her grandmother. Although Celeste was a remarkably youthful octogenarian, Sylvie had noticed that she was beginning to have difficulty getting up from too-soft, too-low sofas and chairs.

She had looked fondly at her grandmother. Behind the old woman's back, she and her sisters referred to their mother's mother as the Queen. Stern, sharp-tongued and regal, Celeste Robichaux did not brook disobedience. But they all knew that beneath the domineering veneer beat a heart that was loving and kind, especially when it came to her four granddaughters. Her generosity was one of the worst-kept secrets in the family.

And the Queen's eyes missed nothing.

"Meeting someone?" she asked in a manner that said it was a foregone conclusion and no denials would be accepted or believed.

The question took Sylvie aback. She had said nothing to either woman beyond the fact that she was going to Maddy's party, and attending parties was something she had done on more than one occasion. For a moment, she thought of brazening it out, the way she would have done as a teenager. But she saw no point to it. Lies were cumbersome things.

Sylvie shrugged casually, checking through her small purse to make sure she had everything she needed. "As a matter of fact, I am." She grinned broadly as she explained, "Your other granddaughters conspired against me and got me a man, *Grand-mère*."

Instead of looking shocked, Celeste made a dismissive noise and waved her finely manicured hand at the information. "I hope they didn't throw away the receipt. Only one use for most men." She glanced significantly at Daisy Rose. "After that…" Her voice trailed off, as if she knew that her meaning was understood.

"My Remy had a great many uses," Anne reminded her mother with no small amount of affection in her voice. Until he was taken from her suddenly four years ago, the genial, outgoing Remy had been the love of her life. No one who had ever met the man had not liked him. He'd even won over her mother, no easy feat.

Both she and her mother had volunteered to look after Daisy Rose tonight while Sylvie went out. Anne had volunteered first, but since her heart attack, her mother insisted on accompanying her almost everywhere, refusing to believe her protests that she was "just fine." Anne knew that the woman meant it out of love, but it still made her feel trapped. Not a condition a woman who'd been her own boss for so many years welcomed.

"Your Remy was the exception that proves the rule," Celeste sniffed, undaunted.

Sylvie had lingered a few moments longer, waiting to see if the air would clear. Grandmother could be cantankerous when she chose and she didn't want anything to upset her mother.

But Anne remained her usual cool, collected self, an attitude that had taken years to hone around the woman who had given her life and the verve to pursue it.

It appeared that war was not to break out tonight. Satisfied, Sylvie had hugged each woman in turn and given her little girl a sound kiss, solemnly instructing Daisy Rose to keep an eye on her grandmother and great-grandmother.

"You can count on me, Mama," Daisy Rose had promised in her almost grown up voice.

Lord, Sylvie thought, what had life been like without Daisy Rose? She couldn't begin to remember. With a delighted laugh, she'd hugged the little girl again, and then, seeing the taxi pull up outside her door, she had taken her purse and her leave.

"Have a good time," were Anne's parting words.

"But not too good," Celeste had called after her, raising her voice. "Daisy Rose doesn't need a little brother or sister yet."

No need to worry about that, Grand-mère, Sylvie thought to herself now, as Celeste's words echoed in her head. The last thing she was looking for was a relationship with Gregory Peck.

Or even Johnny Depp, she added silently, thinking of what she'd said to Maddy yesterday. Her life right now was very, very full. There was no room for anyone else.

They were here, she realized abruptly, finding herself looking up at the hotel's familiar front entrance as the taxi slowed to a stop.

The next moment, one of the valets employed by the hotel was at her door, opening it for her.

"Miss Sylvie, surely you didn't come back to work tonight," Paul said. His dark eyes swept over her appreciatively. Married, with three children and one on the way, the man still had an eye for the ladies, although it was on a strictly "look but don't touch" basis. His wife numbered a voodoo high priestess among her distant relatives, it was rumored, and Paul was not a man who took chances. "Not dressed like this, at any rate. You look lovely."

She smiled her thanks as she handed the cab-driver several bills to cover the fare and a generous tip. "Very perceptive of you, Paul." Sylvie slid out of the cab, accepting the valet's hand. "I'm going out with one of the hotel guests."

Closing the taxi door behind her, Paul smiled. "Lucky guest."

She smiled to herself as she murmured, "We'll see."

THE LAST DATE he had been on was back in college. With Donna. An entire generation had been born and grown up since then, Jefferson thought nervously as he adjusted the light gray silk tie at his throat.

What was he doing here, acting like some single guy, pretending to have a clue? He wasn't single. He was a family man. A family man whose family, through no fault of his own, was no longer as large a unit as it once had been. But family men didn't date.

With a sigh that went clear down to his toes, he put on his jacket and left the hotel room, checking to make sure he had his key card in his pocket.

He hadn't even felt this nervous taking his bar exam, he thought.

Jefferson pressed the button for the elevator. It arrived almost immediately. Getting in, he felt like a condemned man about to walk his last mile. Definitely *not* the way to approach a date.

The elevator doors closed with an unnerving finality. The only way he was going to get through tonight, he decided, was to pretend this was just some kind of work function he was attending. Sylvie Marchand wasn't his date, she was just someone he was escorting. That she was lovely didn't help matters any. On the contrary, it made him feel guilty. As if he were somehow cheating on Donna. It didn't matter that she was gone, that she had been gone for eight years. She was his wife and always would be. When he had said, "Until death do us part," he hadn't meant her death—he'd meant his.

He had no business doing this, no business going out socially with anyone but old friends.

Old friends.

He thought of Blake, who was partially responsible for this. Blake, who was supposed to have been here, lending his support, distracting him. But at the last minute, Blake had called to say that he'd meet Jefferson at the gallery instead. His excuse was that "something" had come up. Judging from the sounds he'd heard in the background, Jefferson figured that what had come up was Blake's libido.

He frowned. It was almost as if the man was trying to prove something to himself. That he was still the stud, the babe magnet he had been all through college. If Jefferson hadn't helped Blake, hadn't stayed up all those nights tutoring him, he would have flunked out of Tulane.

And this was how his friend paid him back, Jefferson thought darkly. Deserting him at the last minute. How the hell had he allowed himself to be talked into this?

Reaching the ground floor, the elevator came to a stop. Jefferson made up his mind. As soon as the last passenger stepped off, he was going to take the elevator back up to his floor, call Sylvie on her cell phone, make his apologies and act like the father of a sixteen-year-old instead of some over-the-hill Romeo.

The elevator doors slid open slowly, almost sighing as they did so. It seemed to him that everything here moved in slow motion.

He didn't belong in New Orleans. He'd outgrown it. His time here was something out of his past, and it was wrong to try to recapture it or even revisit it. Whoever had come up with that old saying about not being able to go home again had been right.

You couldn't just—

Jefferson's breath caught in his throat like a stone. The elevator car had emptied and he was standing alone in the center of it.

Standing and staring at this vision who was looking directly at him.

The doors began to close again. At the last moment, he stuck out his hand, and the doors slid apart again.

His mouth had suddenly gone so dry, he felt as if he'd just gargled with sand.

"Sylvie?" Her name left his lips almost hesitantly.

Sylvie began walking toward the elevator car, curious and maybe a little amused that he hadn't left it yet. "If you're planning on riding up and down in the elevator for a while, we're going to miss the beginning of the dinner," she warned him.

A dimple. There was just the slightest hint of a dimple in her right cheek when she smiled like that. He saw it now as amusement highlighted her face.

And then he came to. Feeling like a dolt, Jefferson quickly put out his hand to stop the doors from closing again. They slid back once more, allowing him to walk out into the lobby.

Sylvie hooked her arm through his as if they were old friends instead of new strangers. "What was all that about?"

He didn't want to tell her that his second thoughts were having second thoughts, or that he'd almost lost his nerve. He didn't even want to admit the latter to himself.

"I, um, thought I left something in my room."

The luminous eyes that were turned up to his face told him she saw right through him. "And did you?"

Looking into them, he found himself getting lost.

It took effort to draw back, to keep from drifting into those eyes and forgetting everything else. "Did I what?"

"Leave something in your room?" she prompted.

It was hard stringing one thought into another when she gazed up at him like that.

"Um, no, I didn't," he finally said, his tongue as thick as that of a first-time offender coming up with an alibi. "My—my wallet's right here."

God, but that sounded lame, he thought, annoyed with his lack of creativity. No one listening to him would have taken him for a six-figure corporate lawyer who could withstand the scrutiny of razor-sharp legal minds bent on taking him down.

But then, none of those sharp minds had ever had a body or a face like the woman beside him. He felt lucky that he could remember his name.

His middle name eluded him.

"Then we're all set to go?" she asked.

She posed the question as if she were deferring the decision—all decisions—to him. Part of feminine southern charm, as he recalled. He had no doubt that beneath the soft, melt-in-your-mouth exterior and lilting voice was a woman who had a resolve of steel. That, too, was part of the southern woman's mystique.

Her eyes were looking straight into his soul. Jefferson roused himself before it was too late. Before he was completely lost.

"Yes, we're all set to go," he echoed.

"Good."

Adjusting the silvery shawl that her grandmother Celeste had worn when she was her age and equally high spirited, Sylvie once again hooked her arm through Jefferson's.

The arm that had been taken hostage was half a breath away from Sylvie's chest, and Jefferson felt his stomach tighten.

"Let's go," she said cheerfully.

As they walked through the lobby to the front doors, Paul was there to attend them. He nodded at Jefferson, but it was obvious that his attention was on Sylvie.

"Will you be wanting another taxi?" he asked, glancing briefly at Jefferson before turning his attention back to Sylvie.

"Absolutely." All but batting her lashes, Sylvie gazed up at Jefferson. "Unless you'd rather walk there."

Jefferson had absolutely no idea where this place was located. Ordinarily, he would map out destinations, but somehow, he'd had a feeling right from the beginning that this evening was not going to fit under any heading he was familiar with.

"How far away is this place?" he asked her.

Sylvie made do with a guesstimate. "About five miles, give or take. In the Warehouse District."

There was no way Jefferson intended to walk that far tonight, not in shoes that pinched. Emily had insisted that he buy a new pair before he left, saying that his comfortable, beat-up ones just wouldn't do.

"A cab would be good."

No more was necessary. Paul's hand went up. Within seconds, a taxicab was pulling up to the entrance. The valet held the rear passenger door open for them. Sylvie slid in first, and Jefferson followed, trying not to crowd her or make any undue physical contact. His knee still managed to brush against her leg as he sat down.

Sylvie leaned forward and gave the driver the address of the gallery, then sat back. Maybe it was his imagination, but she seemed to be sitting even closer to him now than she had been a second ago.

The interior of the taxi felt oddly intimate. That didn't exactly help his resolve to keep this evening on a strictly friendly basis. As they drove, the evening shadows intruding within, the taxicab seemed to grow smaller by the block. And that heady scent Sylvie was wearing surrounded him. He hadn't been able to pin it down yet. All he knew was that it was weaving its way into his senses in less time that it took to begin and end a thought.

His imagination was working overtime tonight, Jefferson told himself. He was going to have to be careful.

The silence inside the cab grew, and he searched his chaotic mind for a neutral topic. The sound of her voice took a moment to register. He realized she was asking him a question.

"So, is it different?" Sylvie repeated.

He didn't have a clue what she was talking about. "Excuse me?"

Sylvie couldn't help smiling to herself. The man

her sisters had set her up with had to be the politest person under the sun. Of late, she'd been teaching Daisy Rose manners, and the little girl was trying very hard to please her. Until this evening, Sylvie would have said that Daisy Rose was the last word in politeness, but this man was a match for her.

"New Orleans," Sylvie clarified. "Do you find that the city's different than you remember it?"

"A little," Jefferson managed to reply. He'd gone sightseeing by himself yesterday, after calling Blake to tell him that he'd arrived. He supposed he could have waited until Blake was available, but he didn't mind doing things by himself. After Donna died, he'd gotten used to doing things alone. And he had wanted to see the city on his own first. "There are some stores I don't remember, and some of the places I used to go are gone now. But for the most part, the old saying's true. The more things change, the more they remain the same."

Sylvie nodded, not knowing how to respond to the cliché. She had an uneasy feeling that her escort was acquainted with a whole host of old sayings. She fervently hoped the rest of the evening wasn't going to continue along the route it seemed to be taking.

The taxicab barely crawled with all the traffic. Jefferson began to wonder if they were ever going to reach the gallery.

Finally the driver pulled up in front of what looked like a huge barn. A pounding beat pulsed through the walls, and Jefferson could almost swear his bones were vibrating.

"We're here," Sylvie announced exuberantly, adding a silent *Finally* to herself. By all reckoning, that had to have been the ten longest minutes of her life.

Oh God, Jefferson thought, getting out behind Sylvie. Was the music going to be this loud all night? He could barely hear Sylvie now and they weren't even close to the front door.

This date, he thought, not for the first time, was a huge mistake.

CHAPTER SIX

IT TOOK JEFFERSON more than a few minutes to ac-
climatize himself to his surroundings. It was a little
like stepping through a portal into another dimen-
sion. Everything inside the gallery was moving at a
much faster pace than that outside its multi-light
bathed walls.

Obviously not everything in New Orleans was
laid-back, he thought.

He looked at the woman in front of him, who'd
been leading the way from the moment she'd
stepped out of the cab. Sylvie seemed right at home
here amid the noise and the milling crowds and the
flashing lights. The woman who had brought him
into this surreal world seemed to thrive on the energy
that was buzzing about the gallery like an electric
current.

Sylvie had been almost subdued in the taxi by
comparison. Here, in the gallery, she was glowing.
She'd come into her own, he supposed, and like a
thirsty flower that had been given water was now,
swiftly and miraculously, blooming right before
his eyes.

He wished the same could be said of him. That the assault on his senses didn't make him want to turn on his heel and race toward the closest exit, hail a cab and go back to the hotel.

Too much.

Those were the words that came to him as he looked around. Too much noise, too much humanity crammed into one limited space. He supposed that in Sylvie's eyes, he was probably dull. He liked quiet evenings, walks along the beach, if there was a beach to be had, long, lingering dinners. He liked to be with a person on a one-on-one basis. The crowd within the gallery definitely did not lend itself to that. If anything, it was more like one on one hundred. You couldn't get to really know a person while enmeshed in a crowd, especially when you couldn't hear a word the person was saying.

But he had signed on for this and he wasn't one to back away from anything, so he was determined to make the best of the evening. Given a choice, he'd prefer that Sylvie didn't think of him as a wet blanket—even if he was a little damp, he mused. But that was because of the lights. They made the gallery hot.

Jefferson loosened his tie and unbuttoned his jacket in self-defense.

Sylvie turned to look at him. Just before she grasped his hand and pulled him into what seemed like the belly of the beast, she flashed a smile that somehow made the whole experience a great deal better. She had a really wonderful smile, he caught himself thinking. The kind that could end wars and send men journeying off on impossible quests.

"C'mon," she coaxed. "I see Maddy."

Her lips were moving, but he couldn't make out the words. "What?"

Sylvie raised her voice. "Maddy." She pointed with her other hand. "I see her."

Maddy. That would be the woman responsible for this cacophonous marriage of sound and people. That would also be the woman Blake was currently seeing, he recalled. So, where there was Maddy, there too would be Blake. At least he hoped so. The thought of a familiar face in this unfamiliar territory heartened him.

"Good," he said, "lead the way."

Another smile. This one went straight up and down his body like dueling bolts of lightning.

A sea of bodies had to be navigated before they reached their goal. Elbows and knees seemed to come at them from strange angles. People were moving, talking, some even dancing, although for the life of him, he couldn't make out any melody, just that continuous beat from the band.

By the time they finally reached Maddy and Blake, Jefferson felt a little like Admiral Perry when he and his party arrived at the South Pole.

Blake looked as happy as Jefferson had ever seen him. It made him wonder what his friend was drinking and if he would mind sharing. As far as liquor went, Jefferson could hold his far better than most, a trait he attributed to both his genes and his height.

Seeing them, Blake beamed, patting Jefferson on the back as if he'd just won some sort of contest. "I see you finally made it."

"Is it always this crowded?" Jefferson asked, doing his best not to shout.

Sylvie shook her head, thinking of some of the other events that Maddy had held.

"No. This is a real homey bunch," she informed him. "When it's crowded, people are flowing out on to the street." She thought of the last event, held in a smaller gallery. People were practically sitting in one another's laps—something else that sparked conversation. "I think Maddy tried to keep the guest list down this time around."

He found he had to concentrate on Sylvie's lips in order to make out what she was saying. It wasn't exactly what he would have termed a hardship.

"Then all these people are crashing the party?" He gestured around the area.

Blake draped his arm over Jefferson's shoulder as he leaned in to Sylvie. "You have to forgive Jeffy. He's used to smaller gatherings—like two."

To Jefferson's surprise, Sylvie looked at him for a long moment, her eyes almost probing into his soul. And then her lips curved into a smile. "Two is all it takes—if it's the right two."

She was coming to his defense. Jefferson didn't know if he felt drawn to her because of that—or pushed away. Did she think of him as someone who needed defending? Maybe he was taking all of this a little too seriously. Everyone here looked as if they had nothing more on their minds than having a good time.

He told himself to loosen up. He'd been on a rigid schedule for so long, he'd completely forgotten how to relax. How to have fun. It suddenly dawned on him why Emily had been so intent on getting him down here. He smiled, remembering. It was "for his own good," that old cliché that parents usually spouted to their kids.

He silently promised Emily to unwind—as much as he was capable of doing.

A waitress dressed in a black tie, white shirt and black slacks with matching vest was working her way through the crowd, holding a tray before her. The champagne glasses on it were swiftly disappearing. Elbowing his way closer, Jefferson snared two and offered Sylvie one.

She smiled her thanks, then lifted her glass a little. "To tonight."

His eyes held hers for a moment. "To tonight," he echoed.

"Amen to that," Maddy declared, swallowing the contents of her own glass. Closing her eyes, the hostess took a deep breath, as if trying to center herself. When she opened them again, she looked more at peace. She smiled at Sylvie. "Thanks for being here." Belatedly, she glanced at Blake and Jefferson. "You, too," she added, then giggled. "I always get so nervous at the beginning of these things."

"Then why have them?" Jefferson asked. It

seemed only logical to him that if something made you uncomfortable and you could safely avoid it, you did. No one was holding a gun to this woman's head, telling her to throw this elaborate whatever-it-was.

But Sylvie turned to look at him with wide eyes, as if she couldn't comprehend what had prompted him to make such a suggestion.

"That's half the fun, Jefferson," she insisted. "The nerves, the anticipation—it's all exciting. You don't risk, you don't gain." She looked to her friend for confirmation. "Right, Maddy?"

The way she described it, Jefferson thought, she made it sound like a life experience instead of a mere party. Although, he amended silently, he doubted if the word *mere* applied here. The last so-called "party" he had gone to with this many people had been a fund-raiser for a nationally known charity. The noise hadn't been nearly this intense or the dancing on the floor as frantic. And as for the music, that had been provided by a five-piece orchestra. Tonight it was coming from a band whose members looked as if they'd fallen headlong into a vat of rainbow-hued paint.

Maddy captured another champagne glass and paused to take a healthy swallow from it before answering Sylvie. "Right."

"Isn't she something else?" Blake whispered in his ear.

"Who?" Jefferson asked, keeping his voice as low as he could yet still reasonably audible. To insure privacy, he'd turned his back on Sylvie for a moment. "Sylvie or Maddy?"

"Maddy," Blake responded with the air of someone who'd thought his reference was obvious. But then he cocked his head, thinking. "Although now that you mention it, your date is pretty hot, too."

"She's not 'mine,'" Jefferson pointed out patiently. He doubted if their paths would ever cross again after tonight. And then he glanced at Sylvie with a discerning eye. "But the rest of your assessment stands."

Blake looked at his fraternity brother with barely veiled annoyance. "Jeez, Jeff, don't sound as if you're analyzing a paper about the devaluation of the American dollar. This is a flesh-and-blood woman you're talking about, for God's sake. Show a little appreciation. From what I hear, guys were always lining up six deep to get her attention."

Watching Sylvie as she talked to one of the other guests, Jefferson could well understand that. There was a wild, yet ethereal quality about her. Half devil, half saint. One well-placed look from her could easily start a fire in any man's hearth.

But that assessment didn't jibe with the facts. "Then what's she doing applying to a dating service?" he asked.

Blake hesitated. "She wasn't, exactly."

Jefferson's eyes narrowed as he looked at his friend. "What?"

Blake seemed to debate with himself a few

seconds, then admitted, "Her sisters put in the application for her."

The information hit Jefferson like a thunderbolt. Sylvie hadn't done this of her own volition, either. She'd been forced into it, just as he had.

That gave them something in common, he realized. And the fact that she'd gone along with her sisters' scheme gave them even more in common. He wouldn't be here if it weren't for Emily.

Jefferson's mouth curved upward at the feeling of empathy he had for this woman.

Sylvie picked that moment to look up at Jefferson. Since he was smiling, her own smile broadened. Maybe the evening wasn't going to be a disappointment after all, she thought. Maybe it just took Jefferson a little bit to come around. And he was kind of cute in a dignified, sophisticated sort of way.

"I've got the best crowd tonight, Sylvie," Maddy was saying. Her eyes seemed to fairly glow as she looked around, Jefferson noticed. Or maybe that was the effect of the lights.

"Do you know all these people?" he asked. It seemed incredible to him that one person could have a sphere of friends and acquaintances this large. But if she didn't know them, what were they doing here? The woman was at least a decade past the age when invitations to a party were passed on by word of mouth, the way they were in high school.

But Maddy's answer made him realize that, to some extent, that was exactly what had happened.

"Well, some are friends, some are people I button-holed at the gallery, others are tourists—"

When he stared at her incredulously, Sylvie leaned in and laughed against his ear. "She's serious."

Jefferson's body braced in response as Sylvie's breath warmed his skin and reduced whatever resolve he had to overcooked oatmeal. He forced himself to focus on what she was telling him. That for the most part, the people here were as much strangers to Maddy as they were to him. It was hard for him to wrap his mind around that. He couldn't conceive of just walking up to a total stranger and asking him to attend a party he was throwing. Why would anyone in their right mind do that?

Maybe that was the way things were done these days. In all honesty, he had to admit that he didn't know the first thing about putting a party together. That had been Donna's domain. Once she died, the reason for parties had come to an abrupt halt.

If she noticed Jefferson's shock, Maddy gave no indication. "And here's the best part," she said with enthusiasm. "I managed to get some of the biggest critics in the state to attend. They're here for the Mardi Gras season."

She rattled off the names of several people along with their credentials. There were a couple of theater critics, one from New York, and several columnists whose articles were syndicated in major newspapers across the country. There was even one notable movie critic who had been around for the past twenty years.

Jefferson was surprised that this particular critic would come to an event like this. They must be close to the same age, which Jefferson supposed, made him the one who was out of step.

"There are people here who have never agreed on anything in their lives," Maddy concluded, as if that was a positive thing.

"And you like this," Jefferson asked, trying hard to make sense of her enthusiasm.

Maddy looked at him as if she couldn't believe he was even asking the question. "Yes!" Every fiber of her being seemed to resonate in the single word.

But Jefferson was still trying to understand. Where he came from, confrontations were things to resolve, not encourage. "You like having people argue."

Maddy shook her head. "Not argue—discuss, debate."

In his book, those were just synonyms for *argue*. But he had a feeling that his was not the reigning view, so he dropped his line of questioning. This was a whole different world for him.

"You're allowed, you know," Sylvie whispered against his ear.

There it went again. Her breath, skimming along his skin. This time, it made the hairs on the back of his neck rise up. There was no point in trying to talk himself out of it. He was definitely attracted to this woman.

"Allowed?" he echoed, turning to look at her. He wasn't sure he followed her meaning. Right about now, he understood what Alice must have experienced after falling through the rabbit hole and meeting up with a host of creatures that seemed to come from another world.

"To disagree with her," Sylvie explained.

That seemed a little general, he thought. "About what?"

She spread her hands wide, as if to encompass the entire area and everyone in it. "About anything. And with anyone," she added. "That's what this evening is all about, Jefferson. To get people with different points of view, from different walks of life gathered in a room. You present them with the same kind of stimuli and then have them share their reactions."

Cocking her head, Sylvie studied his expression and decided that she was not getting through the way she wanted to. He became her challenge.

"Okay, for instance…" Taking Jefferson by the arm, she drew him over a little way so he could see the far wall more easily. "Take those three paintings over there…" She pointed toward them.

Having her pressed against him like this made it difficult for Jefferson to keep his mind on the conversation and not the soft curves that were making an impression on his body, in more ways than one. He did his best to focus. "Yes?"

Sylvie looked at him for a reaction. She had deliberately hung a Jackson Pollock painting in between the two very subdued pastoral scenes she had contributed from the gallery. Since Jefferson appeared almost impassive, she prodded. "How do they make you feel?"

He was by no means a critic. He knew what he liked and what he didn't like, without being able to attach a name to the period, style or, except for the most famous, artist.

"Feel?" he echoed.

Sylvie was nothing if not patient. She felt a little like a shepherd, guiding a sheep to a field of clover. "Yes, seeing them grouped like that. How does that make you feel?"

Jefferson was quite sure this was not what she was after, but he gave her the only answer that came to him. "As if there's too much art in one small space."

Sylvie looked at him for a moment, her expression unreadable. He could only guess what was going through her mind. That she'd made a mistake agreeing to come with him and that she was going to bale at the first opportunity.

And then, to his surprise, she laid her forehead against his shoulder and laughed.

"Honest. Good." When she raised her head again, she looked up at him. "But it doesn't evoke anything else? In here." Lightly, she tapped her fingers against his chest. "You don't feel something?"

Yes, he was feeling something, but it wasn't because of the paintings. It was the effect of her close proximity. Because she was sharing the same air as he was, perhaps even the same breath. And because she was stunning, both to look at and to be with.

"Yes," he told her quietly, so quietly that she had to lean in even closer to hear him. He could smell her shampoo, something light and herbal. It didn't surprise him. "I feel something."

Her eyes meeting his, Sylvie caught her breath. For a moment, just a single moment, time felt as if it were standing still. A very unusual occurrence for her. For most of her adult life, she'd been accustomed to feeling that time was zipping by on a motorized skateboard.

Something was happening here. What, she wasn't sure, but it was a nice something. That was good enough for her.

Sylvie's smile began in her luminous eyes, reaching her lips less than half a heartbeat later. Taking him prisoner without firing a shot, he thought.

"Maybe I do, too," she replied.

The moment was gone when a man came up behind them, laced his arm around Sylvie's waist and nuzzled her neck before declaring, "Knew I'd find you here, Sylvie. Can't have an event like this without Sylvie Marchand."

Something oddly primitive raised its head within Jefferson's chest. He felt strange and uncomfortable, both with himself and the situation. He disliked the man instantly, even though he was not given to snap judgments or hasty reactions. A desire arose— to place himself between Sylvie and this guy, whoever the hell he was.

He felt, Jefferson realized with a start, territorial. He looked down to see if his arms had suddenly lengthened, causing his knuckles to scrape along the ground.

The sound of Sylvie's voice had him looking up again.

"Bryce," she was saying, "this is Jefferson Lambert. He's a high-profile criminal lawyer back in Boston," she announced cheerfully.

Because he had a poker face, Jefferson managed to keep the fact that Sylvie's introduction had completely floored him a secret. High-profile criminal lawyer? Where had she gotten that idea?

He was just about to correct the description when he felt a hard poke in the ribs. Glancing to his left, he saw the look in Blake's eyes. His friend had elbowed him with the clear intent of silencing him.

"We went to college together here," Blake told Bryce as he extended his hand to him. "Tulane. I'm Blake Randall."

"Are you a criminal lawyer, too?" Bryce asked.

"Why, do you need one?" Blake countered.

Bryce laughed heartily, not realizing that Blake was leading him away.

Looking over his shoulder, Blake gave Jefferson the okay sign. The look in Blake's eyes urged him to continue the charade.

Jefferson had never been comfortable lying. And now that he knew Sylvie thought he was a criminal lawyer, he wondered if there were other things about him that had been misrepresented.

Suddenly, the evening, the performance art event, all began to make sense. He was going to have a very long and serious talk with Emily when he got back. Good intentions only bought you so much grace. He

knew she'd probably tried to make him sound more
with it and cool, but that had wound up matching
him up with someone under false pretenses.

The next moment, Sylvie was grabbing his arm
and guiding him away. "I'm glad your friend ran in-
terference for us. Bryce would have wound up mo-
nopolizing the whole evening."

"Somehow," Jefferson said, looking at her, "I sincerely doubt that." The woman clearly could hold
her own, and in a duel of wits, he was beginning to
doubt that she had a close match.

Sylvie took his words as a compliment and
laughed softly.

Despite the noise, the sound traveled straight to
his gut, rooting there.

Maybe that talk he was going to have with Emily
didn't have to be such a long one after all, he
amended silently.

CHAPTER SEVEN

"Do you dance, Jefferson?"

Jefferson turned to look at the woman at his side. He wasn't quite sure if he had heard her correctly.

For the past forty-five minutes, he'd allowed her to take the lead, which she'd done with enthusiasm, going from one grouping of paintings to another. Each had a cluster of people before it, discussing, sometimes rather passionately, the meaning behind the arrangement.

The whole process left Jefferson cold. As far as he could tell, the paintings had been placed in particular groupings for no other reason than to tease the minds of those who searched for some kind of hidden meaning in every shadow that crossed their path and every raindrop that fell.

He kept his thoughts on the matter to himself, however. He had no desire to get into a debate with Sylvie. It wasn't as if they were laying down the foundations of a future life together. This was only one evening—granted, a unique evening—in his life, and when he looked back on it months from now, it would undoubtedly stand out as one of the strangest.

At the same time, it was one of the most interesting evenings he'd ever spent. Sylvie Marchand was definitely one of a kind, and spending time with her was not without its merits.

So when she'd turned to him suddenly, just as his mind was in danger of glazing over after listening to a very opinionated little man whose manner was as pretentious as the toupee he wore, and asked him a question out of the blue, Jefferson was not sure he'd heard her right.

Stalling a second as he tried to refocus his attention, he cleared his throat. "Excuse me?"

"Dance," Sylvie repeated, turning her body so that she deliberately blocked out Harland T. Baker, the critic from *Art Today* magazine who'd annoyed her because he hadn't allowed another person to get a word in edgewise. "You know," she elaborated, her amusement growing, "move your feet in time to music, whether from some sort of inner melody or from an outside source."

"I know what *dance* means." Ordinarily, he might have taken offense that he was being poked fun at, but there was something about the way she looked at a man, something about the southern lilt of Sylvie Marchand's voice, that took the edge off and made him want to smile in return. "I just wasn't sure I heard you correctly, that's all," he explained. He glanced around the immediate area. Driving through the country, he'd encountered towns that had less people than were crammed in here tonight. "This isn't exactly the reading room of the Boston Public Library."

She'd noticed his slightly pained expression when she turned toward him. He hadn't said a single word in the past forty-five minutes. Not about any of the paintings nor the people who wanted to discuss them.

"What's the matter, Jefferson? I thought you liked art." His application had said that he enjoyed, among other things, modern art and stimulating conversation. The performance event they were attending offered both, and yet the man looked as uncomfortable and out of place as a shepherd at a presidential inaugural ball.

"I like art," he told her mildly, not adding that some of the things he'd seen tonight did not come under that heading as far as he was concerned. "I just don't like arguing about it."

She was leading him somewhere again, he thought. But where? At least that pompous windbag wasn't following, he noted. The man with the bad toupee was still holding court at the last grouping.

Sylvie seemed to have a destination. This time, she was drawing him over to one end of the gallery where several other couples were dancing—if you could call it that, Jefferson thought. From what he could ascertain, the couples were more or less hanging on to one another in one spot, occasionally moving their feet as if to keep time in case anyone was paying attention.

In his book, that wasn't dancing, but at least the music was slower now, without that relentless beat.

"Not arguing, exchanging opinions," Sylvie

countered as she turned around to face him. "Dance with me?"

She'd obviously taken the answer to her earlier question to be yes, he thought. Maybe dancing was something Emily and Blake had listed as one of his interests on the application. Either way, he felt more at home here than he had standing in front of those paintings.

Jefferson slipped his arm around her waist and tucked her hand beneath his, bringing it up against his chest. He began to sway with the music. Her hips shadowed his, moving with the rhythm. He found it almost primal. Something within him came to attention and then went on red alert.

Sylvie smiled up at him. "I can feel your heart beating," she murmured.

"Good, that means I'm still alive." He guided her past one of the couples. "Nothing kills a party faster than a dead guest."

She laughed, and he could feel the sound rippling up through his chest. "You know, you're nothing like your application."

He could readily believe that. Emily was nothing if not creative. He should have thought of that before going along with her plan, he realized. "That could be because my application was written by a sixteen-year-old."

Sylvie cocked her head. Most men wouldn't have been secure enough to admit that. "Your inner child?" she guessed.

"My inner daughter," he corrected, "and I say

inner because she's probably going to be grounded for the rest of her life when I get back."

Well, there was something that hadn't been covered on the dating service's application, she thought, surprised. "You have a daughter."

He couldn't tell by her expression if that bothered her, or if she was just asking to make sure she'd heard him. "Yes, I do. Her name's Emily."

Sylvie wondered what else hadn't been put on his form. He didn't look like the type who cheated, but she'd learned that looks could be deceiving. One of the men she'd been involved with had had a wife and family he'd conveniently forgotten to mention until she'd all but stumbled across them in the park.

"Do you have a wife to go with your daughter?"

A sadness stirred inside him. It always did when he thought about his life without Donna. "Had."

"Oh." She heard the sadness in his voice. Was he still in love with the woman? Pining after her? "I'm sorry. Divorced?"

He laughed softly to himself and shook his head. "If only."

Her eyes narrowed. "I don't follow."

Jefferson glanced down at the open-toe high heels she was wearing. "Actually, you follow very nicely," he told her.

It had been a long time since he'd been on the dance floor. Dancing was one of those activities that he'd always liked, one he'd taken to naturally after his mother taught him the fundamental steps of ballroom dancing just before he entered high school. Aeons ago.

A fondness warmed him as he remembered dancing with his wife. Donna had been a wonderful partner everywhere but on the dance floor. Her movements there had been stiff and awkward. She'd never known how to loosen up, how to let the music flow through her and take her over. In contrast, the woman now in his arms felt as if she would allow music to take her everywhere.

"But as to my meaning," he continued, easily gliding along the limited floor space, "if I were divorced, then I would have an ex-wife, but I don't."

Sylvie looked up into his eyes. And knew. "Your wife died."

Funny how that word still managed to take a bite out of him. "Yes."

"Recently?" That would go a long way toward explaining things, Sylvie thought, sympathy flooding her veins.

The smile on his lips was self-deprecating. And sad. "Feels that way. But no, not recently. Donna died in a car accident on the way to work eight years ago. Eight-car pileup. Made all the local papers." He couldn't look anywhere without seeing her mangled silver BMW. Without imagining her crushed body within. "She was a lawyer, like me."

"Criminal?" Sylvie asked, remembering what was on the form.

"No, family law." As he danced with Sylvie, he debated his next words, then decided that he had absolutely nothing to lose by telling her the truth. Lies made him uncomfortable and they also had a very unfortunate habit of growing out of proportion when you were least able to deal with them. He might never see Sylvie again after tonight, but he didn't want to leave a lie in his wake. "I'm not a criminal lawyer, Sylvie."

The admission caught her off guard. "But your application—" And then she stopped and laughed. "More of Emily's handiwork?"

She'd been paying attention, he thought. Otherwise she wouldn't have caught his daughter's name. "I'm afraid so."

She took a breath, processing this newest tidbit. If he wasn't a criminal lawyer, then what was he? "Was anything on the application true?"

"Well, I am a lawyer. A corporate lawyer. But as for the rest of it, I really can't say," he told her honestly. "I didn't get to see the application before it went out. I didn't even know it was going out," he admitted. "Otherwise—"

"You never would have let her submit it." It didn't take an Einstein to guess that.

"No." He reconsidered his words. After all, he was here. He hadn't been tricked into coming. "But I never would have allowed her to misrepresent me as some kind of high-profile high roller."

Rather than looking disappointed by his admission, she was smiling. Her *eyes* were smiling, he amended, taken by the sight. Even with the lights changing color every few seconds, bathing them in greens and golds, purples and blues, he found himself captivated by the look in her eyes, the expression on her face.

He was still holding her. And liking it.

The band, he realized, had finished playing the slow song, and the next number was wild and frantic. For a second, he stopped moving and stepped back.

He didn't know how to dance to this, Sylvie thought. That was all right, it didn't matter. She liked what he'd been doing before.

"Don't stop," she coaxed, taking his hand and placing it back along the gentle swell of her hips. She slipped back into the pocket of space he had created for her against him. Her hips began to sway again, as if the song they'd just been dancing to had never stopped. The look on her face told Jefferson she was all set to continue slow dancing with him, moving to the music in her head.

Jefferson paused for a moment longer, letting the rhythm that was now pulsing hard and fast throughout the gallery settle into his system. With a nod, he took her hand and began to dance to the beat.

Stunned, unprepared, Sylvie stumbled for a second. She stared at him as she fell into step. He'd surprised her. Again. "This isn't an old dance."

"No," he agreed amiably, "it's not." He had no idea what the song was called, or what heading it could be filed under. But he was good at imitating what he saw, and there were people around him dancing. The natural rhythm he'd been born with did the rest.

Within moments, the other dancers began to back away, giving them room. Watching them with appreciative expressions.

Sylvie felt exhilarated, improvising and then laughing as Jefferson half twirled, half swung her around the floor. By the time the number finally came to an end, she realized that she was very close to breathless. Was that because of the dance, or the man? She couldn't say. All she knew was that she felt extremely alive.

Applause rose from all sides.

Sylvie laughed. "That was wonderful," she exclaimed, hugging him. "You are a man of many surprises, Jefferson Lambert." Still trying to catch her breath, she rose up on her toes and impulsively kissed him.

The laugh in her throat faded away as she found herself the recipient of yet another, far greater surprise.

She'd only meant to brush her lips against his. But one swift pass led to another. And another. Each time, the contact was a little longer, a little deeper. What began as less than a kiss blossomed until she felt it engulfing her.

Reacting, not thinking, Sylvie threaded her arms around Jefferson's neck and drew her body closer to his, giving in to whatever it was that was happening here.

The kiss deepened until it had no beginning, no end.

And the longer she kissed him, the more she wanted to.

Finally, she stepped back.

Her head was spinning, her pulse seemed to have taken over her entire body and she was throbbing from top to bottom. The last time she had felt this way, Daisy Rose had come along nine months later. But unlike Shane Alexander, Jefferson wasn't trying to overwhelm her with his sexual prowess. He was just kissing her. Nothing more.

Nothing.

The word echoed in her head. *Everything* was more like it.

"Lots of surprises," Sylvie heard herself saying again in a breathy tone. She realized suddenly that she was running the tip of her tongue along the outline of her lips, savoring the taste of him.

Well, he hadn't been prepared for that, Jefferson thought almost numbly. Soldiers were expected to make their beds so that a quarter could be bounced on top of their blanket. That was how taut everything felt inside of him right now. Stretched so far it was in jeopardy of breaking.

Yet he couldn't remember when he'd felt so alive.

He hadn't seen the kiss coming. And he certainly hadn't been prepared for his own reaction to it. He hadn't kissed any woman but Donna since he was in his first year at Tulane.

Once Donna came into his life, she was all he needed. And after she was taken from him, he never had the desire to connect with another woman. Never felt any of the urges that his colleagues liked to spend so much time talking about on Monday morning. Sex was a three-letter word that he had agonized over only when he thought of Emily being confronted with it. Until now.

Her breath sufficiently recovered, Sylvie smiled

at him as she threaded her fingers through his. She indicated the tables she'd helped set up yesterday. They were to the far left of the gallery's central viewing area. Elegant glasses were set beside finely embossed paper plates. Nothing was conventional where Maddy was concerned.

"Come," she coaxed, drawing him toward the tables. "I think I just heard Maddy signaling everyone to come eat."

Maybe she had, Jefferson thought. All he'd heard was the sound of his own heart, beating loudly in his ears.

He took a breath and held it, silently telling his pulse to stop scrambling, his heart to settle down and his breathing to return to normal—whatever that was. Doing his level best to appear as if that kiss had not cut him off at the knees, Jefferson allowed her to lead the way to the tables.

As they approached the designated dining area, he saw that Blake was looking their way. Looking *his* way, Jefferson realized. And grinning. It was the kind of grin that fairly shouted *I told you so.* Blake couldn't have looked prouder of himself if he had single-handedly invented the wheel *and* discovered fire in the space of an afternoon.

Just because he'd danced with Sylvie—and kissed her—although technically, she had been the one to kiss him—didn't mean this was a match made in heaven. Or even in New Orleans. As far as he was concerned, it wasn't really a match at all, just a case of opposites attracting. Temporarily.

"Saved two places for you," Blake told them, rising from his chair.

He gestured vaguely toward the two empty chairs to his right without taking his eyes off Jefferson. To spare himself, Jefferson deliberately took the second chair, holding the one between himself and Blake out for Sylvie.

The look on Blake's face told him that gloating had merely been postponed until the earliest opportunity.

"So the dancing part is true, if somewhat understated," Sylvie said to Jefferson as she took her seat. When she saw Jefferson's eyebrows draw together in a puzzled expression, she elaborated. "On the application, you put down— It said," she amended, since he'd told her he hadn't filled it out, "that you could dance."

She seemed to remember an awful lot of what Emily had written down. "Did you memorize the application?" he asked. That he had never seen it was making him increasingly uncomfortable. What else had Emily said about him that might trip him up later, or make him look like a fool?

The smile on Sylvie's lips was impossibly sexy. "Just the parts I found appealing."

She leaned back as a server with a steaming tureen of jambalaya stopped by her chair to spoon the fragrant mixture of rice and seafood into her side dish. Directly behind her was a tall, thin young man with no hips who was offering servings of blackened ribeye. Next came an assortment of vegetables, all darkened with a Cajun sauce.

Sylvie shook her head just as the server began to transfer a portion of the vegetables onto her plate. "Hate vegetables," she confided to Jefferson. She waited until the small parade had served Jefferson. "But now," she told him, picking up the thread as if she hadn't abruptly stopped, "we're going to have to start from the beginning."

He wasn't sure just where she was going with this. "The beginning?"

"Yes." With knife and fork in hand, she studied the ribeye, deciding where to make the first cut. "Since, by your admission, the application I have in my possession is mostly a work of fiction, you're going to have to tell me all about yourself."

Jefferson had never been comfortable talking about himself. He shrugged vaguely, searching for a way to begin a new topic. Blake was no help. He'd turned his attention to Maddy. Their heads were close together and they were whispering—sharing something intimate and amusing, judging from the way Maddy laughed in response.

"Not much to tell," Jefferson finally replied.

Somehow, Sylvie thought, she had her doubts about that. Until he had danced with her, she would have been willing to believe that perhaps he was just a one-dimensional kind of guy. But no one who had moves like his could possibly be one-dimensional. She'd bet her private art collection on that.

"I don't believe you," she informed him, her voice coaxing.

He had a feeling that she could probably charm bees out of their hive if she set her mind to it.

"C'mon, Jefferson, give. Your daughter got your height and your weight right and I'm assuming she knows when you were born."

He was about to ask her what year Emily had put down, but then he stopped. It occurred to him that Emily might have wanted to fudge that, seeing that Sylvie was more than ten years younger. And their profiles had been matched. But then, he reminded himself, he'd already made up his mind not to lie. This was not the time to go back on his decision.

"That all depends," he said.

"On what?"

"On what she put down."

Sylvie thought for a moment. "It said that you were born in 19—"

The last two numbers were lost as the gallery suddenly, without warning, went black.

CHAPTER EIGHT

NERVOUS LAUGHTER ECHOED in the darkened gallery, chasing away the eerie silence that had blanketed the room seconds ago as guests attempted to adjust to what they assumed was yet another part of the entertainment.

Sylvie shifted in her chair. She didn't mind the dark as long as she could still make out forms and figures. But this was pitch black and it imprisoned her.

"Hey, Maddy, I thought the object was to get people talking, not groping." She aimed her words in the direction where Maddy was sitting. "I can't see anything."

"Join the club," someone from the crowd chimed in.

Sylvie suddenly became aware of a small, steady beam of light coming from her right. When she turned, she saw that Jefferson was holding what appeared to be a tiny flashlight attached to a set of keys. The illumination it provided was disproportionate to its size.

Her uneasiness began to fade. She felt as if the

cavalry had arrived. Leaning into him, she told Jefferson, "You are turning out to be one very handy man to have around."

The appreciative note in her voice warmed him more than he would have expected. "Emily's gift to me two years ago for Father's Day. In case I got home after dark and the porch light wasn't on."

"Remind me to send her a thank-you note." He looked a lot more sexy in this light, Sylvie thought. Or was that the champagne talking? She'd had two glasses, and ordinarily, that wouldn't affect her. But maybe, this once, it had. The man beside her wasn't her type for so many reasons, and yet...

Focusing on the immediate problem, Sylvie turned toward her friend. "Tell them to turn the lights back on, Maddy."

Maddy was already on her feet. The exasperated look on her face told Sylvie this hadn't been planned.

"Damn straight I will," she declared.

Here and there tiny flames of light began appearing as several people at the tables took out their lighters or struck matches to see. An uneasiness was telegraphing itself through the crowd.

Any second, Sylvie thought, panic might set in. She was having trouble banking down her own growing anxiety and she wasn't given to that kind of thing.

When Jefferson rose to his feet, Sylvie thought that he was going make his way to the exit before the situation in the gallery turned uncomfortable or tempers flared. The sudden power failure was a damn good reason to call an end to an evening that he probably found less than thrilling anyway. But to her surprise, Jefferson raised the flashlight he was holding just above his head and addressed the other guests.

"Everyone?" He raised his voice when only a few people looked his way. "Everyone, can I have your attention? There seems to be some kind of technical difficulty at the moment—"

"I'll say," a voice from the darkness cracked with less than gracious humor. Other people were heard to mumble far more caustic comments.

Jefferson ignored the grumblings. Instead, he went on speaking in a soothing, authoritative voice. "Security is being dispatched to see what the problem is. It's probably something minor. It usually is. There's no reason to panic."

"Can we panic after they find out what the problem is?" that same person asked. Snickers echoed in the wake of his question.

Jefferson never missed a beat, addressing the query as if it had been seriously asked. "That all depends on what they find out."

The voice in the darkness had no response. The faces of those closest to Jefferson looked satisfied and placated by his assurance.

Sitting down again, Jefferson turned to look at Sylvie and his hostess. There was sheer gratitude on Maddy O'Neill's face, as if he'd just saved her from pitching over a steep cliff.

What he saw on Sylvie's face was a great deal

more complex. All he knew for sure was that when she looked at him, he felt as if he was standing on quicksand and sinking fast.

Well, there was just no going with first impressions, was there, Sylvie thought, studying Jefferson with re-kindled interest. She made no attempt to disguise the fact that he had impressed her a great deal. She would have expected him to hang back or leave, not take charge. But that was exactly what he'd done. There was no way for him to know about security—he'd just said it for the crowd's sake. He could think on his feet, she thought, another admirable quality.

Slow down, Syl. No need to give him a ticker tape parade yet.

Aloud, she said, "I guess you're the type who rises to the occasion."

On her other side, Blake laughed. "The guy comes through every time," he told her. "Usually when you least expect it."

Jefferson shrugged. He had little use for compliments. "I just didn't want to see mass panic take over," he told Sylvie. "Crowds can get ugly without meaning to."

Maddy leaned over and put her hand on his, pressing it. "I owe you one," she told him. "Would you mind doing me one more favor?"

The gentlemanly thing would have been to give an unqualified "yes," but he'd learned never to jump into something feet first without knowing if it was cement or Jell-O. "And that would be?"

"Could you light the way for me so I can get to

the back room?" Maddy asked, then lowered her voice. "So I can get that security guy to do what you just told the crowd he was doing."

"It'd be my pleasure," Jefferson said as he rose again.

He was aware that Sylvie had popped up beside him like a jack-in-the-box. He couldn't decide if it was because she liked his company or because she really didn't like being in the dark alone. Either way, she was coming with him. He could live with that, he thought, suppressing a smile.

IT WAS A BLACKOUT. A massive power failure that not only affected the Warehouse District and the French Quarter, but sent long, thick, probing fingers into the surrounding areas.

The media got wind of it almost immediately and played it up as a colossal disaster in the making. Conflicting reports began coming in as rival stations raced to be the first to present new information for a news-junkie public. The truth was that no one knew at this point just how much of the French Quarter was actually without power.

Luc Carter knew that fate was on his side. This was the break he'd been waiting for. He'd been planning a power failure, and one had been delivered with perfect timing. The sugar he'd poured into the generator's fuel line would put a major crimp in the Hotel Marchand's Twelfth Night celebrations. Richard and Daniel Corbin, the people he really worked for, would be pleased.

He'd taken a major chance, though. Charlotte had sent him off to get flashlights and he'd detoured by the furnace room where the generator was kept. He should never have risked it. One of the maintenance men was already on the scene to investigate, and Luc had hurried past, grumbling about the shortage of flashlights. Returning to the scene of the crime was something an amateur would do, but that pretty much described Luc.

The Corbin brothers believed he was working for them for the part ownership they'd promised him once he managed to bring financial ruin to the Hotel Marchand, forcing Anne to sell to them. What they didn't know was that Luc was in this for personal revenge. But in fact, his enthusiasm for his plan was starting to wane.

No, if he was accurate, his desire to wreak havoc on Anne Marchand and her family had begun to weaken awhile ago—the moment he'd begun to get to know the four Marchand sisters, who, unbeknownst to them, were his cousins, and the genteel, kind-hearted woman who was his late father's older sister.

He couldn't help but wonder what Anne Marchand would say if she knew he was Pierre's son. Would she be surprised? Would she welcome him? Or would she turn him away? It was something he wasn't going to find out. Not if he stuck to his plan, which had dovetailed perfectly with Richard and Dan's.

Luc had idolized his father. Not that Pierre had

been around much when Luc was a kid. After giving him his name and his charm, Pierre Robichaux had abruptly left Luc and his mother one day after Luc had just turned six. Left him with memories of a charismatic man who could light up a room with his smile. Who could fire Luc's imagination with stories of his youth in New Orleans.

It was only later that he'd learned that the man he adored had feet of clay. That Pierre was fatally addicted to gambling and to alcohol. And to women. Even so, Luc refused to allow that knowledge to diminish the way he felt about his father.

When Pierre had finally returned to his wife and son, a broken, dying man, a heartsick Luc had searched for a target to fix his anger on. Pierre's stories of how his own mother, Celeste Robichaux, had turned her back on him had provided one.

Just before his father died, he'd extracted a promise from Luc to reclaim his rightful share of the family fortune. Pierre had also wanted him to tell Anne that he had always loved her. But Luc had silently vowed to make his grandmother, his aunt and any other Robichaux pay for what had happened to his father. Intuitively, Carla Carter desperately tried to talk her only son out of harboring such bitter feelings. She tried to make Luc see that his father had been a liar and a cheat who had not done an honest day's work in his life.

Luc refused to listen to his mother, refused to hear a single word spoken against the father he'd worshiped and adored. Troubled, confused, he'd left the country shortly after the funeral. After traveling for a while, he'd ended up in Thailand, working for a hotel chain run by Dan and Richard. It turned out the men, half brothers, were seasoned grifters. When they learned that he wanted to go to New Orleans, they transferred him to their hotel in nearby Lafayette.

The brothers were intent on buying out a prime hotel, but not at a prime price. Through contacts in the industry, the Corbins had sniffed out the Hotel Marchand's precarious financial situation and set their sights on acquiring it. To drive down its value, the reputation of the hotel had to be compromised. A plan was devised to undermine the hotel's good name and make things so difficult for Anne that she wouldn't be able to make payments on the hefty mortgages that existed on the property. Eventually, as the hotel became a liability, she would have to sell.

Because of his background working in hotels, Luc easily secured a position as the concierge. Weaving himself into the tapestry of everyday life at the Hotel Marchand, he made himself indispensable. And so began a game of cat and mouse. He'd already engineered some minor things to upset guests. Things like embedding slivers of glass in the hotel towels and deleting reservations from the computer. The towels had been discovered by the head of security before any harm could be done, but the vanishing reservations were a black mark on the hotel's record.

And now the damaged generator.

He should feel like celebrating, but he couldn't help thinking of Anne Marchand's warm smile and Daisy Rose's impish grin.

The only one in the family who could make him remember his initial vow was his grandmother. Celeste Robichaux was every bit as hard a woman as his father had told him she was. She rarely came to the hotel, but when she did, she swept through like Catherine the Great, treating everyone around her as if they were serfs. Most of the time, Celeste looked right past him as if he didn't exist.

With a mother like that, Luc thought, no wonder his father had left New Orleans.

Luc could hear music and happy voices coming from the courtyard. He repositioned the pile of flashlights in his arm and headed for the lobby. Maybe he'd underestimated the magic of New Orleans. Even in total darkness, the party went on.

THE MOMENT THEY WERE OUTSIDE the gallery, Sylvie realized that what they were experiencing was more than just a minor inconvenience. There were no lights at all in the street.

Thoughts of disasters immediately sprang to mind.

Without thinking, Sylvie grasped Jefferson's hand, holding on tightly, the unconscious fear she was struggling to hold at bay radiating through her fingers.

She'd been in New York City when the Twin

Towers fell. Although she was all the way across town at the time, the memory of that day was still vividly imprinted in her mind. Over time, she'd managed to bury it beneath so many others, but it was quick to surface at the slightest provocation.

Fear strummed across her nerves, refusing to dissipate. She turned toward Jefferson. "Do you think this could be—?"

She didn't have to finish. He could hear it in her voice, see it in her eyes. "Probably not" was the best he could offer her. He wouldn't just glibly assure her that this blackout was not part of something bigger. But the odds, he liked to believe, were against that. "Why don't you call home?" Jefferson advised. "It might make you feel better."

She didn't ordinarily need reassurance. She usually had no trouble keeping a positive outlook, but for some reason, the darkness had taken away her confidence. She didn't like feeling this way.

Sylvie had her cell phone out and was pressing buttons before Jefferson had completed his suggestion.

It took three rings before anyone answered. The seconds seemed to stretch out forever. Sylvie could feel impatience mounting within her.

As soon as the ringing stopped, she said, "Hello, Mama?"

"You sound breathless, Sylvie. Is your date chasing after you, or are you chasing him?"

Not her mother, she thought. Anne Marchand's tongue was not nearly as tart. "*Grand-mère*, is everything all right over there?"

"Other than the fact that your mother is boring me to death with her poor skills at the chessboard, I would say that everything is all right." A hint of curiosity slipped into the older woman's voice. "Why do you ask?"

"Sylvie, what's wrong?" It was her mother on the phone now. Sylvie surmised that Anne must have taken the receiver from her grandmother, who could be heard grumbling in French in the background.

"Nothing's really wrong, Mama." She didn't want her to worry unnecessarily. Ever since Anne's heart attack, Sylvie had felt very protective of her mother. As she talked, she began to twist a lock of her hair, a habit she'd had since she was a girl. "We've just had a power failure here at the gallery where Maddy's having her performance event and I wanted to make sure you and *Grand-mère* and Daisy Rose weren't sitting in the dark, too."

"The lights flickered here earlier, but everything seems to be fine now," Anne assured her. Then she drew her breath in sharply.

"What?" Sylvie demanded. "What is it?" Jefferson was looking at her quizzically. "Did the lights go out?"

"No, but I just realized this blackout should have hit the hotel. We have power here, but the hotel is a few miles away. I'd better go down to check and see—"

Sylvie cut her off. "Mama, you stay where you are. Daisy Rose needs you. I'm already out—I'll go to the hotel. If there is a power failure, I should check to make sure the paintings are all right, especially the ones on loan from the museum—and *Grand-mère's* Wyeth," she reminded her mother. Sylvie had been thrilled when Celeste agreed to allow the gallery to display the priceless Wyeth for a few months.

"Oh my Lord, the paintings."

Sylvie tugged impatiently on her hair, annoyed with herself. Someday, she was going to have to learn to censor her words before she spoke. "Don't worry, nothing's going to happen to the paintings. I'll sleep with them if I have to. Kiss Daisy Rose for me," she added, just before she ended the conversation.

Jefferson looked at her. "Daisy Rose?" He hadn't intended to eavesdrop, but since Sylvie was less than a foot away, it would have been difficult for him not to hear everything.

"My daughter," she explained. She saw mild amusement flicker across his lips. "What?"

Slipping his arm around her, he moved her out of the way as several people hurried from the building. He hadn't seen Blake since he'd left his former roommate and Maddy at the generator. Knowing Blake, he would probably use the blackout to his advantage somehow. "I guess mine wasn't the only daughter who didn't make it onto the application."

That surprised her. Just what were her sisters trying to do?

"It didn't say that I had a little girl?"

He shook his head. "No. How little?" he asked. He missed Emily being little. When she was

younger, she had hung on his every word and hadn't
yet developed her independent streak—the one that
seemed to be growing every day.

More people emerged from the gallery, stum-
bling a bit in the dark. Jefferson guided Sylvie off
to one side, narrowly avoiding a collision with a
man who looked like he was more at home on a
football field than in a gallery.

"She's three—and two handfuls," Sylvie added
fondly.

It was easy to see that her daughter was the joy
of her life.

"I left her with my mother and grandmother."

He thought of Emily and what a challenge she'd
been during the babysitting years. He grinned.
"Think they'll be safe?"

Sylvie laughed. The night air was cool and she
pulled her shawl tighter around her shoulders. "Obviously you've never met my grandmother. She
could send an alligator into therapy." As she spoke,
she was pressing the button on her cell phone keypad
to connect her to the hotel's front desk. When the
number of unanswered rings grew, she found herself
becoming more uneasy. She tried Charlotte's cell
phone. This time, a message said the user was out
of the calling area.

Sylvie frowned. "Someone should be answering."

"Why don't we get back there and see what's
going on?" he suggested.

This was her responsibility, not his. "You don't
have to come with me."

"Yes, I do." And then he smiled. "I'm staying there, remember?"

"Right. Sorry." How could she have forgotten that? Was she really that flustered? "I'm not usually this disconnected."

His eyes swept over her. "From where I'm standing, you seem very connected." This time, rather that taking her elbow, he offered her his arm. "Let's see about getting a cab."

Sylvie nodded as she slipped her arm through his.

Finding a taxi was easier said than done. An army of cabs was on the street tonight, but either they were already occupied or someone beat the two of them to the door.

The minutes were ticking by. Sylvie felt herself growing more edgy. She couldn't very well call her mother back and tell her to go to the hotel in her place. The woman did not need this kind of stress.

"Maybe we should walk," Sylvie suggested. She saw him looking down at her shoes. She had on open-toe high heels that made her seem several inches taller than she was. "I know the hotel is a few miles away, but it's better than standing here."

He had his doubts about that, and even greater doubts about Sylvie making the journey in the shoes she was wearing. Searching for an alternative, Jefferson looked around. That was when he saw it. A horse-drawn carriage standing across the street. He'd thought carriage rides were only available within the French Quarter. Apparently not.

Impulsively, he grabbed her hand and dashed across the street.

"What are you doing?" she asked, breaking into a sprint to keep up. Horns blasted around them as they zigzagged between cars. With the lights out, traffic had snarled badly. No one was in a patient mood.

"Seizing the moment," he cried.

She was about to protest that she had a hotel to get to and didn't have time for an adventure when she saw what had attracted his attention. Her mouth dropped open.

"How much would you charge to take us to the Hotel Marchand?" Jefferson asked the driver, a wizened old man who practically seemed to disappear into the coat he was wearing.

The driver squinted at him. "I'm on my way to the stables. Time for Apples to rest. Besides, I don't know where that hotel is."

Sylvie found that a little odd—the hotel had been around for decades—but she quickly volunteered the address. The driver shook his head so hard, his top hat slipped. He made a grab for it and pushed it back on.

"Sorry. I don't remember things as well as I used to," he apologized. "Me and Apples here just go around the area, nothing more. Less competition."

Jefferson wasn't about to give up. "Tell you what, why don't you sit in the back with Miss Marchand and I'll drive you there."

Distrust was stamped on the man's gnarled features. "And steal my carriage?"

"I don't want your carriage or your horse," he insisted. "The lady and I just need to get back to the hotel. You keep an eye on the route we take and you can make your way back." Jefferson gave him an encouraging look. "Sharp man like you should have no trouble, right?"

"Right." But he didn't sound sure.

Taking out his wallet, Jefferson extracted five twenties and pressed them into the man's hand. The driver stared at the money. His scowl faded a little. Finally, he shoved the bills deep into his pocket.

"Okay. But nothing fancy. Apples doesn't like surprises."

"Nothing fancy," Jefferson promised. Turning, he started to help Sylvie into the back, but she shook her head.

"I'm riding up front with you," she informed him. Drawing closer to him as the driver got into the back, she lowered her voice. "You sure you know how to drive one of these things?"

Jefferson climbed up into the seat reluctantly vacated by the driver. Leaning over, he offered Sylvie his hand. "My grandfather had a horse ranch in Wyoming. I spent a lot of summers there."

Sylvie wrapped her fingers around his and climbed up into the seat beside him. "So, you're a cowboy, too, besides being a crowd controller and a lawyer. I must say, I'm impressed, Jefferson."

He liked the way she said his name. "Nothing to be impressed about," he demurred.

A lawyer, a cowboy—and modest, too, Sylvie

thought. She caught herself smiling as they began to make their way along the crowded street. *Not a bad combination.*

CHAPTER NINE

THE SOUND OF THE HORSE'S HOOVES hitting the cobblestone street leading up to the Hotel Marchand echoed in the night air. Sylvie had no idea why that seemed romantic to her, especially given the nature of the situation, but it did. Her vulnerability made her uneasy. There was no point in having her emotions stirred up by this man. This was a date, nothing more. By this time next week, they would be separated by several states.

But the funny little glow she was experiencing remained.

They'd had one uncertain moment when the impatient driver of a low-slung sports car leaned on his horn. Apples had seemed about to rear. Sylvie had grabbed on to her seat, envisioning herself spilling out onto the sidewalk. Miraculously, Jefferson seemed to anticipate the horse's reaction. Leaning forward as far as he could, still holding the reins tight, he talked the animal into a calmer state.

As the carriage approached the hotel, Sylvie looked at Jefferson with unabashed respect. He might resemble Gregory Peck, but she was becoming convinced that the man was hiding a large letter *S* just beneath his shirt.

"So now you're a horse whisperer," Sylvie had said.

He'd merely shrugged. "Just doing what needs to be done, nothing more."

They didn't make men like this anymore, Sylvie thought.

And then her attention was redirected to the hotel. Usually well lit, the Hotel Marchand now looked like a candle whose wick had all but been extinguished. Through the windows Sylvie detected the flickering shadows cast by lamps and candles.

Why hadn't the emergency generator kicked in? she wondered. The old-fashioned hurricane lamps were mostly for decor, but obviously they had been pressed into service. Charlotte was nothing if not innovative.

"Oh, God," Sylvie murmured, more to herself than to Jefferson, "the guests aren't going to be very happy about this."

He glanced at her. "The hotel can't be held responsible for the blackout," he said. "And neither can you or your family."

She doubted that there were many people who'd agree with him. People who'd spent their hard-earned money on vacations, only to find less-than-perfect conditions, were usually eager to point fingers.

Sylvie shifted in her seat, impatient to get inside. "No, but we'll pay the price for the bad impression they're going to take back home." She pressed her lips together, remembering what Charlotte had told her just the other day. "This is one of our best weeks so far," she explained. "We still haven't recovered completely from Katrina."

Just shy of the hotel's entrance, Jefferson brought the carriage to a stop. Paul was still on duty. He hurried over, eyeing the horse and carriage skeptically. His eyes shifted toward Sylvie. "That's kind of a different horse power than I'm used to, Ms. Marchand."

"Relax, Paul, you won't be parking him," Sylvie promised. The valet extended his hands toward her, and she let him help her get down from her perch. Feet safely planted on the ground, she glanced over her shoulder at Jefferson. "Mr. Lambert commandeered the carriage when it looked like all the taxis were spoken for."

Jefferson could have sworn he'd heard a note of admiration in her voice. He smiled to himself. It felt good being someone's knight in shining armor. Turning in his seat, he handed the reins he'd been holding to the little man seated in the passenger seat behind him.

The carriage driver eagerly clambered onto his perch. Back in his rightful place, he nodded curtly at Jefferson.

"Not a bad driver," he muttered. "You ever want to do this professionally, look me up. Maybe we can work something out."

Jefferson grinned. "I'll keep that in mind. Never know when I might need a new career."

The next second the man was off, as if he'd suddenly reconsidered his offer and was afraid that Jefferson might take him up on it.

"Odd little man," Sylvie commented, watching the carriage make its way through the press of cars trying to negotiate the narrow streets of the French Quarter.

"He probably wasn't too comfortable having someone handling his horse," Jefferson said as he took her elbow and guided her toward the revolving door.

There were candles or hurricane lamps on every available flat surface in the lobby. Under different circumstances, Sylvie might have found this incredibly romantic. Right now she had business to attend to, however.

"You don't have to come with me, you know," she said to Jefferson. Maybe older men were still into chivalry, which was nice, but she didn't want him feeling obligated.

Jefferson merely smiled as they made their way through the lobby. "Trying to get rid of me?"

Actually, she was beginning to really enjoy his company as well as appreciate it. She'd always admired resourceful people. "No, it's just that this doesn't exactly come under the heading of a typical date." *More like above and beyond the call of duty,* she added silently.

She looked around for Charlotte, but only a few people were milling around the lobby or talking to the desk clerks.

Music floated in from the courtyard, where the revelers at the Twelfth Night party seemed to have regrouped. It made her think of the musicians who played to calm the patrons on the sinking *Titanic*. *Cheerful thought,* she admonished herself.

"In my opinion," Jefferson was saying, "neither did that gathering we just came from." At least, it wouldn't have been his choice for a typical date.

She glanced at him, picking up on his disapproving tone. "I take it you don't like performance art."

Honesty, he'd already decided, was the right way to go. "I don't really know what the heck that is," he confessed.

A small furrow formed just above the spot where his eyebrows were drawn together. It made him look kind of sexy, Sylvie thought, in a scholarly sort of way. "Something else Emily put down?"

He laughed, glad she was being a good sport about this. Glad, too, that Emily had talked him into coming here. "Apparently."

His cell phone rang just as Sylvie spotted Charlotte. He excused himself while Sylvie tapped her sister on the shoulder. "Sylvie, what are you doing here?"

"Riding to the rescue." Charlotte had no idea how accurate that statement actually was. If it hadn't been for the horse and carriage Jefferson had commandeered, the two of them would still be back at Maddy's gallery. "Seeing if you could use any help."

Relief washed over Charlotte's features. She'd been trying to keep all the balls in the air and it felt like they were going to come crashing down on her head at any moment.

"God, could I ever." She placed her arm around her sister's shoulder, vaguely aware that there was someone with Sylvie and that he was talking on a cell phone. "The emergency generator's not working and I'm worried about the paintings in the gallery," she said bluntly. "I think we've got the rest of the hotel covered as best we can."

There'd been no one at the other end of the line when Jefferson answered the call. Probably the service was overloaded. Turning toward Sylvie, he pocketed his cell. "Have you had trouble with thieves before?"

Charlotte looked at him. She wasn't accustomed to being questioned by people she didn't even know by name. "And you are?"

"Charlotte, let me introduce you," Sylvie cut in, suddenly realizing Charlotte had no idea who Jefferson was. Sylvie knew she had a habit of sailing through life, confident that everyone was on the same wavelength as she was. "This is Jefferson Lambert, the man you, Melanie and Renee thought I needed to go out with," Sylvie told her. "Jefferson, this is my sister Charlotte Marchand."

Jefferson took Charlotte's hand into his. Obviously preoccupied by her concerns for the hotel, Sylvie's sister didn't seem to be processing the information. "The dating service," Jefferson added, hoping to clarify things for her.

"Oh." Charlotte's eyes suddenly widened. *"Oh."*

The second "oh" had a far more appreciative quality than the first as her eyes quickly swept over the man standing beside her sister. Charlotte was accustomed to making judgments quickly and she found that she liked what she saw. The word *solid* echoed in her brain. That word had never occurred to her before when she'd been confronted with one of Sylvie's dates. But then, most of them had looked as if they'd fallen off a truck transporting scruffy protesters. Especially the one who'd fathered Daisy Rose.

This man looked as if he held a respectable position in society. Maybe he was a professor at a small-town college. She took a second to congratulate herself.

Sylvie inwardly cringed. God but Charlotte was transparent. You would think that a woman who wasn't exactly successful in the romance department herself wouldn't be so fixated on trying to match up her younger sister.

"You were saying something about the paintings in the gallery, Charlotte," she prompted.

"Right." Coming out of her momentary mental revelry, she addressed the immediate problem. "I'd really appreciate it if you could take one of the staff and set up camp in the gallery for the night. God knows the security team is overtaxed right now. Mac seems to have disappeared on me, along with Julie," she said, referring to the head of security and her own administrative assistant. "There's a sofa in the back room. You could take turns catching a few winks."

Sylvie gave her an exasperated look. "I know there's a sofa, Charlotte. I'm in the gallery every day, remember?"

Charlotte decided to use the blackout to Sylvie's advantage, and slid another look toward Jefferson. "On second thought, I'm really going to need all the staff. Perhaps Mr. Lambert could—"

"No, he couldn't," Sylvie cried, jumping in before her older sister succeeded in completely humiliating her.

It didn't take a brain surgeon to see where this was going. Or to foresee the eruption that was about to occur.

Jefferson cut in before strained nerves caused tempers to flare. "I'll be happy to keep you company and take a turn standing guard over the gallery's paintings."

"I knew I liked you the minute I saw you," Charlotte told him.

Sylvie knew her sister meant well, but it still irritated her to have Charlotte meddling in her life. "And we all know what a sterling judge of character you are."

Charlotte gave her a sharp look, obviously picking up on the reference to her ill-fated marriage. "Everyone's entitled to one mistake." And then she smiled. "And I'm sure that Mr. Lambert is not a second one."

"As a matter of fact, Jefferson earned two merit badges on the way over here," Sylvie told her. "One for quieting a potentially panicky crowd at the gallery and another for bringing me here by horse-drawn carriage when we couldn't find a taxi."

Charlotte paused a second to see if Sylvie was putting her on. The look on the man's face told her that her little sister was reciting chapter and verse. "I do like a man who thinks on his feet," she said.

But could he think when he wasn't on his feet? Sylvie mused. An image formed in her mind, one that involved bubbles, hot running water and scented candles.

She tossed her head, her hair bouncing over her shoulder. "You can have your turn with him tomorrow. Tonight, he's mine. Let's go, Jefferson."

Jefferson inclined his head toward Charlotte, silently taking his leave, then lengthened his stride to catch up to Sylvie. "Am I being passed around, Sylvie?" he asked, amused.

She was trying to circumvent several boisterous tourists discussing something in a language she took to be German. "What?" Sylvie realized that he might have taken her exchange with Charlotte the wrong way. "Oh, no, I'm sorry if it sounded that way—"

He raised his hand before she could continue. "That's okay. I was only pulling your leg. You looked as if you needed to lighten up for a minute."

The soul-wrenching sigh came before she could bank it down. "I've needed to lighten up for the past year."

"Things that bad?"

Sylvie immediately felt guilty. She had a great deal to be grateful for. "No, they're not. And it's probably not fair of me to grumble. It's just that there're times I feel like I'm losing who I am."

"And who *are* you, Sylvie?"

They were almost at the lobby entrance to the gallery, but Sylvie stopped. The question hit too close to home for her to simply shake it off. And Jefferson was standing much too close to her, Sylvie realized as she looked up into his eyes. Ordinarily, she wouldn't mind that, especially since the pull she felt toward him seemed to have been growing in intensity ever since they got into the back of the taxi earlier this evening.

But there was something more. Something that made her feel uncertain. It was almost as if she were standing on the brink of something new, something she hadn't experienced before.

She was too old to jump into anything feet first. Carefree women did that kind of thing, not mothers of three-year-olds.

Sylvie drew in a breath. "A woman who needs to get to the art gallery and set up camp. You hungry?" she asked abruptly.

They hadn't had a chance to sample any of the food that had been served at Maddy's event because the power failure hit. After that, adrenaline had been pumping too hard for Jefferson to even think of eating. Now, however, his appetite announced that it was alive and healthy. And waiting to be appeased.

"Yes."

"I'll see if I can get someone in the kitchen to conjure up something for us to eat as soon as I call my mother and tell her I'm spending the night here." Taking out her cell phone, Sylvie quickly placed a

call to her mother, then spent the next five minutes
assuring Anne that everything was fine, despite the
fact that the power was still out. "This is just pre-
cautionary, Mother. Kiss Daisy Rose for me and tell
Grand-mère not to drive you too crazy."

"Too late for that," Anne laughed softly. "You're
sure everything's—"

"I'm sure, Mother. Bye." With that, she ended the
call. "Next, food," she murmured.

Crossing to one of the courtesy phones, Sylvie
picked up the receiver and pressed a button. Her
eyes swept over the lobby as she waited for someone
to pick up on the other end. So far, no one looked as
if they were losing their temper, and the sounds of
music and laughter drifting in from the courtyard indicated the party had kicked back into high gear.

"Room service," a weary voice finally said
against her ear.

Sylvie, recognizing the voice, snapped to attention. "Allison?"

"Yes?"

She'd gotten the heavy-set, amiable young assistant pastry chef whose passion was to create sinfully
delicious desserts. "Allison, this is Sylvie Marchand.
Do you think you could throw together a couple of
ham sandwiches, two slices of your terrific apple pie
and a couple of cans of soda—any kind—and send
them over to the art gallery?"

"The art gallery?" the woman echoed quizzically.
"Isn't it closed at this hour?"

"Usually," Sylvie agreed. "But Charlotte wants

me to stand guard in case someone decides to make off with the paintings."

The idea of thieves breaking into her gallery was unnerving, even though she pretended to be blasé about it. The hotel had been home to her and her sisters when they were growing up. She couldn't think about the possibility of thieves invading her safe haven.

But in light of what happened in the aftermath of Katrina, she couldn't take any chances. So she would stay in the gallery overnight and ease Charlotte's burden. Superwoman Charlotte looked as if she was going to have a nervous breakdown if one more thing went wrong for her. Everyone had a breaking point, and Charlotte seemed close to hers. As her sister, this was the least Sylvie could do for her.

Especially when her guard duty companion was growing more attractive to her by the moment.

"I'll bring it over myself," Allison promised.

She didn't want to put the woman out. "You don't have to do that. I'll come get it."

"It's easier if I do it," Allison countered. "It's a bit chaotic here. There are still people in the restaurant who seem to think this is a great dining adventure. I've already called the electric company twice to find out how long it's going to be before they finally restore power."

"And?"

Allison laughed dismissively. "I can't get through. Looks like everyone else in the French Quarter wants to know the same thing I do."

Sylvie shrugged. The shoulder of her dress slid down. Absently, she tugged it back into place. "It'll be over when it's over, I guess," she said philosophically.

There was no point in agonizing over the situation. Hanging up, she saw that Jefferson was studying her, his expression amused. He looked sexy when he smiled like that, she thought, wondering if he knew. Probably not. He struck her as a completely unselfconscious man. Unlike Daisy Rose's father.

Now where had that come from? She hadn't thought, really thought, about Shane Alexander in a long time. "What?" She realized Jefferson had asked her a question.

"Are you sure you and Charlotte are sisters?"

"I'm sure. She's the type A in the family. Took after my mother." Between the two of them, they could probably run the entire hotel by themselves, Sylvie figured, if the rest of the family would allow her mother to be that foolish.

"And you took after your father?"

"Probably." It was a compliment to be compared to the father she'd loved, a man who was liked and admired by almost everyone he met. And then she shivered. "I'd hate to think I took after my grandmothe.r"

"Why's that?"

Only someone who had never met Celeste Robichaux could ask that question. "*Grand-mère* has a tongue that can slice people in half at thirty paces."

Taking out her keys, she unlocked the glass doors leading into the gallery. There was no need to disarm the security system. The power failure had done that for her.

The gallery, long and narrow, took up two floors. A spiral staircase connected the floors, and the open concept gave the gallery an airy, spacious feel.

Glancing around as she made her way to the back, she noted that everything looked to be all right. No one else was here. She hadn't expected otherwise.

"Personally, I think Charlotte's overreacting. The electricity'll probably be back up in a matter of minutes." Even as she said it, she flipped the light switch. Habit, she thought ruefully as the sound of the empty *click* mournfully testified to the futility of the act.

She found candles she kept for evening events and placed them in containers along one counter, lighting them as she did so.

"Let there be light," she murmured.

The effect was hopelessly romantic, she thought. Or maybe she was still reacting to feelings that had been born at the other gallery. On the dance floor. She attempted to shake herself loose of their influence, wanting to be mistress of the moment, rather than have the moment own her.

Reaching the back room, she took off her shawl and dropped it over the sofa before turning to face Jefferson. There wasn't all that much space available in the small room. "You really don't have to stay here," she offered tentatively.

"What?" He pretended to look at her incredulously. "Leave now and miss out on a ham sandwich and a piece of terrific apple pie?"

"Not just any ham sandwich." Playing along with him, she pretended to take offense on behalf of the absent kitchen staff. "A thick, juicy ham sandwich that's guaranteed to melt in your mouth." She grew serious. "It's like taking a bite of heaven."

Just like kissing you, he thought. "And how many bites of heaven have you had?"

"A few," she countered, looking at him.

What was there about tonight? she wondered. Why was she suddenly craving company? Specifically, why this man's company? Had she been unusually lonely lately? Unsatisfied with this life she'd cut out for herself? Okay, she had a host of new responsibilities, but she'd already begun the transformation three years ago by becoming a responsible mother and now she'd added responsible daughter to her résumé. No big deal.

Maybe big deal, she amended. Since coming back home, she'd felt at times like a bird whose wings had been clipped.

She looked up at Jefferson, her breath lodging in her throat. Funny thing was, right about now she couldn't really say that she minded having her wings clipped.

What was that all about?

Melt in your mouth. Her description echoed in Jefferson's head. He could just as easily apply those words to Sylvie. There was something about this unorthodox woman whom Fate had placed in his path that seemed to be weaving itself under his skin, into his senses.

Was it just because he hadn't been with a woman since Donna died?

Whoa, back up a minute, he ordered himself. He wasn't about to be with anyone now, either. That was the kind of excuse an adolescent used to justify doing something that was reckless and out of character. That kind of behavior was all in his past.

All right, he amended, all in *Blake's* past. Jefferson had been the one who walked the straight and narrow. And that was exactly what he intended to do for the rest of the evening. Be true to his own character. Be true to the memory of his late wife. One unguarded moment, one exquisite, unscripted kiss did not a downfall make.

Not unless it was a kiss with one hell of a kick to it.

Unfortunately for him, that was exactly the way he would have described the kiss he'd shared with Sylvie Marchand as they were leaving the dance floor. Remembering it made his knees weak, a condition he was completely unfamiliar with.

He found himself gazing at her, urges and desires suddenly surfacing from out of nowhere. Vibrating within him. Clamoring for freedom. For release.

Was it just him, or was it growing dimmer in this back room where he was standing with her? And smaller. The room was definitely growing smaller.

Just then, a knock sounded on one of the doors.

Room Service had arrived.

CHAPTER TEN

"WE'RE IN HERE!" Sylvie called out.

Jefferson took a step back from her, feeling slightly awkward, like someone caught doing something he shouldn't have been doing.

If he noticed anything out of the ordinary, Rick, the young waiter Allison had sent, gave no indication as he made his way through the gallery.

"Some night, huh?" he asked cheerfully, walking into the back room. Glancing around, he crossed to the desk. Most of the work space was taken up by the computer and uneven stacks of mail, but he managed to find a flat surface and set the tray down. "Too bad this didn't happen on Halloween. Then we could have told guests the power failure was all part of the celebration. Most people are being good sports, but there're a few real complainers out there."

Sylvie felt terrible for Charlotte. Disgruntled guests were the last thing she needed.

Sylvie removed the lid from the plate of sandwiches. "How are things in the kitchen?"

"Well, the stoves are gas, so we managed to get them going," Rick answered. "But Robert's worried about the things in the freezer going bad. He's not too happy the generator broke down."

He wouldn't be, Sylvie thought. Robert LeSoeur, the executive chef of Chez Remy, was gifted but demanding—of himself and everyone else involved in keeping the restaurant's multi-star rating.

Sylvie wondered what had caused the generator to malfunction in the first place. "Tell Allison I said thank you for sending the tray so fast."

Rick took that as his cue to withdraw. *"Bon appétit,"* he said, and hurried out of the small room. His footsteps receded, and the doors rumbled back into place as he closed them.

Jefferson had taken the opportunity provided by the waiter's appearance to put as much distance between himself and Sylvie as the room allowed. All in all, it wasn't a great deal. The sofa and small desk and chair took up most of the room, leaving little space to maneuver. This was definitely not a room to comfortably accommodate two or more people. Unless they were all pencil thin and on a strict diet of berries and water.

As he moved to take a sandwich from the tray, Jefferson glanced down at the desk and saw the framed photograph of a pretty little redheaded girl with incredibly lively eyes and an infectious smile. Had he not heard Sylvie mention having a daughter, he would have thought he was staring at a photograph of Sylvie as a child. *The apple doesn't fall far from the tree,* he mused, picking up the photograph and looking at it more closely.

Jefferson held the framed photograph toward Sylvie. "Is this your daughter?"

About to go back out to the gallery to make certain everything was where it should be, Sylvie retraced her steps back into the office. She took the frame from his hands and smiled, looking down at Daisy Rose as if she were seeing the photograph, the child, for the first time in a long while. At times, when she got wrapped up in her day, Daisy Rose would melt back into the tapestry of her life. She would forget just how precious the little girl was to her. How lucky she was to have her daughter in her life.

"Daisy Rose," Sylvie murmured, more to herself than in acknowledgment of his question.

Jefferson could hear affection in every syllable. There was something incredibly appealing to him about a woman who so obviously loved her child.

Without fully realizing it, he felt a bond growing between them. "She's as beautiful as her mother."

Sylvie looked up and flashed a smile at him as she placed the photograph back on her desk. "Did you say your daughter was a teenager?" she asked.

"Emily's sixteen going on forty," Jefferson said. And some days, too much of a handful for him, he added silently. "Enjoy your years with her," he advised. "They go by too fast." He nodded at the photograph she'd just replaced. "At three, you can still tell them what to do."

Sylvie laughed. There were days when Daisy Rose made her think of a pint-size little old lady. An *opinionated* little old lady.

"Obviously, you've never met my Daisy Rose."
She took the napkins from the tray and placed one on
his side of the desk. Sympathy nudged her. They
were both paddling canoes through the same
churning waters. "Not easy being a single parent, is
it?"

No, he thought, it wasn't, although he suspected
that Sylvie might have an easier time of it than he did,
since her child was the same sex as her. And from what
he gathered, she had a good support system in place,
surrounded by her family the way she was. He'd had
Donna's mother Sophie for emergencies, but for the
most part, he'd had only himself to rely on. There had
been times when he was sure he wasn't going to make
it. But somehow, he always managed, due, in no small
part, to the fact that Emily was a great kid.

As he watched Sylvie set out their dinner, he
found himself wondering about her. There'd been
nothing on the form to indicate she'd been married.
All it had said was that she was single.

Was she widowed, like him? Was she still nursing
a wound that refused to heal? Empathy flooded
through him. "When did you lose Daisy Rose's
father?"

Setting the tray aside, she looked up, a flicker of
humor in her expression. "I never had him." Because
she had a feeling he stood on ceremony, she picked
up his plate and offered the sandwich to him.

Jefferson hardly noticed the sandwich with its
thick cuts of ham. Sylvie had all of his attention as
he took the plate she handed him. "Excuse me?"

Sylvie laughed, shaking her head. "You have just *got* to be the politest man I have ever met," she commented. Then, in case he thought she was dodging the question, she explained, "Daisy Rose's father and I were never married."

Like someone venturing over a fence, then seeing a sign clearly marked "Do Not Trespass," Jefferson swiftly, if not smoothly, retreated. "Oh, sorry. None of my business."

Most men would have pried, feeling they deserved answers because they were investing their time in a woman. That he didn't impressed her.

"No," she agreed, "it isn't." And then she grinned. "But I'll tell you anyway."

He waited, curious, while she took a bite of the sandwich and finished chewing and swallowing.

"He was a rock musician—on his way down, actually, when I met him. Shane Alexander of Lynx." She looked at him to see if the name meant anything and thought she saw a flicker of recognition. "He could be very charming when he wanted to, of course, and I know I should have been a little smarter than I was, but I fell for his act, which was, sadly, all it was. Just an act." But she was too grateful to have Daisy Rose to lament the past. "Man didn't have much going for him upstairs, but he sure did know how to rock my world in the lovemaking department." About to take another bite of her sandwich, she saw that Jefferson had stopped eating. "Am I embarrassing you, Jefferson?"

Yes, she was. But it annoyed him that he was so

transparent. He had a poker face when it came to arguing cases in a boardroom or the courtroom, but for some reason, he couldn't get it to function outside his professional life. Her remark just underscored how different he and this sprite of a woman were.

Jefferson shrugged. "You're just being honest."

Sylvie had always been in tune with what people thought. Sometimes it was only after the fact, which was why she'd been on the receiving end of heartache so often, but she could usually read people pretty well. And Jefferson had just avoided answering her. "That's not what I asked."

"I'm not accustomed to people being so honest," he hedged. "I'm a lawyer," he reminded her, the corner of his mouth twitching just enough to make her wonder if he was putting her on.

Amusement filtered through her. She really did like this man, she thought. And she was attracted to him. She made a mental note to find a way to repay her sisters without coming straight out and saying thank you. If she did that, they'd be impossible to live with.

"Don't lawyers tell the truth?"

"Certain versions of it," he allowed. He popped the tab of the soda can and foam fizzled onto the lid.

Sylvie finished her sandwich, then said, "I didn't realize there were several versions of the truth."

"There are several versions of everything," he assured her.

And right now, Jefferson thought, the truth was

that Sylvie was making the food he was eating stick in his throat as if it had been doused in glue.

The hunger he'd felt had passed, now that he'd eaten the sandwich, but it was replaced with another type of hunger, one he had not fed for a very long time. One he had been fairly convinced had died years ago due to lack of attention.

Jefferson had never been interested in sex just for the sake of sex, even as an adolescent. First he had to feel something for the person he was with. His mind had to be invited to the banquet before his more basic interests could attend.

"Oh, really?"

She moved aside her empty plate and smiled seductively at him, enjoying his reaction. Enjoying her own reaction to him. Sylvie moved closer, aware of the heat coming from his body. Drawn by it.

"So if I said something like, 'I feel very attracted to you right at this moment, Jefferson,' that could be interpreted in several different ways?"

He couldn't take his eyes from her. Couldn't move if he'd wanted to. And he wasn't all that sure that he did want to, even though he had a feeling he was about to get hit by something with the force of a runaway train.

"Yes," he heard himself say.

A smile crept into her eyes, feathering out to the rest of her features. "Give me one interpretation."

He could feel her breasts against his chest as she took in a breath. Could feel a need unfurling within him. "I can't."

Her amusement made it hard for her to keep a straight face. Her desire made it equally hard not to just throw herself into his arms and see what happened. "Why not?"

He took a breath, seeking to steady himself. He succeeded. Outwardly. "Because my mind has stopped functioning."

The admission delighted her. "Why, Jefferson, I think that must be one of the nicest compliments I've ever been given."

"Wasn't meant as a compliment," he responded. "It's the truth."

Sylvie had been with her share of men, and for the most part, they were given to fabrications, even if they weren't all smooth talkers. This man was a whole new experience for her.

"Haven't had much practice at flattering women, have you, Jefferson?"

Like a man in a dream, Jefferson saw himself placing his hands on the soft, inviting swell of her hips. It just seemed like the natural thing to do, if only to assure himself that she was real and he wasn't having some strange, enticing dream.

"No."

Sylvie felt a shiver travel up her spine in response. Who would have thought that honesty could be so sexy?

"Good, I like that," she murmured. "No bad habits to unlearn. Nothing for me to try to decipher."

He could feel her breath, sweet, enticing, whispering along his face as she spoke. His stomach had tightened and he knew without a doubt he wanted her.

But women, for the most part, were a mystery to him. He didn't want to be guilty of misreading the signs, of acting on things that he only imagined were true.

When in doubt, ask. In the long run, it was simpler that way. "Sylvie?"

If he didn't make a move soon, Sylvie thought, she was going to jump him. A woman could only be so strong. "Yes?"

"Are you coming on to me?"

She could have laughed. The man was an innocent. And yet so damn virile it set her teeth on edge.

"As hard as I can." Sylvie pressed her lips together as she looked up at him. She could feel her body priming. Yearning. "How am I doing?" she whispered.

Had he been holding anything, other than her, he would have snapped it in two. Meltdown, he thought, was close at hand. "You are a difficult woman to resist," he confessed.

She raised her chin slightly, her eyes never leaving his. "Then I have a suggestion."

Despite the seriousness of the situation, he grinned. "Don't resist?"

And then Sylvie laughed. He found the sound hopelessly exotic.

"You read my mind," she said.

He pulled her closer. So close that their heartbeats mingled. She cocked her head, an amused, slightly quizzical expression on her face. He wondered if it was just a facade. If beneath everything, she felt as shaken by what was happening as he did.

"I have to take some initiative here," he told her.

How charmingly old-fashioned, she thought. Despite the Boston address, this man's roots were definitely those of a Southern gentleman caller of yesteryear.

"Men don't have to anymore," she told him.

"Some things," he told her, bringing his mouth down to hers, "don't have to change."

The moment his lips touched hers, she knew. It hadn't been a fluke, Sylvie thought. That lightning she'd felt coursing through her veins earlier this evening when she'd kissed him hadn't just happened because of the moment. It had happened because of the man.

And he had only grown more appealing as the evening progressed.

She supposed that he was the kind of man people described as the "strong, silent type." He would have fit right in to the era of the quiet hero who came riding into town, trying to keep to himself but forced to take charge and save the day because no one else would step up.

He was definitely stepping up.

Excitement pulsed through her as she leaned her body into his. Delicious sensations assaulted her, warming her limbs. Sylvie wrapped her arms around his neck, savoring the very taste of him.

He made her head spin.

She'd teased him about his lack of romantic entanglements, but the truth was, she'd been auditioning for the part of vestal virgin herself recently. She'd been too busy raising Daisy Rose, running the art gallery at the hotel and forging alliances with local artists to even have a fleeting relationship with any man, much less one of substance.

But this man was a man of substance. There was just something about him—the way he talked about his daughter, or asked about hers—that told her, Here is a man who is not afraid of the word *forever.* A man to rely on.

There was a bonfire going on within her now, the flames rising higher and higher. For a man of substance, he could certainly kiss. Contact had instantly aroused all the appetites dormant within her. All the hungers, the desires, the passions that had been safely tucked away ever since she'd become a mother suddenly surged to the surface.

She hung on for dear life. Exhilarated. And more than a little scared.

The deep kiss gave way to more frantic ones. Quick, fleeting kisses that aroused, teased, promised. As his mouth roamed her eyes, her cheeks, the hollow of her throat, Sylvie felt as if someone had lit a Roman candle inside of her. It threatened to go off.

And then she felt his fingers gently coaxing her dress from her shoulders. She had to steel herself to keep the shiver of anticipation banked down. For reasons she couldn't begin to fathom, it almost felt as if this was the first time for her. The first time she'd ever made love.

Eagerly, she began to tug at Jefferson's clothing. She fought the urge to rip it off his body with her teeth. As it was, she was shaking inside as she undid buttons, pulled his shirt out of his pants and made short work of the latter. She had been right. The clothing he wore in no way hinted at the muscular body beneath. He was sculpted.

Her heart hammered. She could almost feel it vibrating in her body as desperation to touch him flowed through her. She wanted to touch him and be touched by him. To have his hands claim what she had already given to him.

Her breathing had grown audible. Funny how such a simple sound like that could set him off, Jefferson thought. He felt as if his knees were buckling even as strength surged through him and he slipped off her bra and panties.

There was no way, when the evening began, that he had thought it would end like this. Here with Sylvie. Bedding the woman wasn't what he'd had in mind.

Now it was the *only* thing he had in mind.

That, and making certain that he pleasured her. Because that was all tied up with his own sense of satisfaction. Making it enjoyable for her would make it enjoyable for him. He'd spent his adult life making certain that whenever he and Donna made love, her pleasure came before his own. It was just the way he was wired.

But things had changed since he was married. And he had a feeling that the woman he was with was far more experienced in the ways of pleasure, both receiving and giving, than he was.

Was he going to disappoint her?

He didn't know, but he did know that this was no time for self-doubt.

He went with his instincts, exploring her body as if he'd just entered a sacred place.

Slowly he caressed her, moving his hands gently along her curves as if one wrong move would cause her to break. With each pass of his hands, the heat between them soared to sizzling, and as his mouth explored her soft skin, Jefferson felt desire threatening his control. Carefully, slowly, he eased her over to the sofa and lay down beside her.

A small sound escaped her lips. He stopped, looking at her, afraid he might have hurt her.

"It's cold," she explained breathlessly. "The leather. Against my back."

He grinned. "I'll see what I can do to fix that." He slid his hands beneath her and drew her closer.

Sylvie twisted beneath him, stealing his breath away. All the systems that he'd thought had been cut off were up and running and about to fire on all cylinders.

Linking his hands with hers, Jefferson nudged her thighs apart with his and then slipped into her. Her legs locked themselves around his torso, and he felt oddly at peace even as a frantic energy seized him.

He was completely filled with the sight, the taste, the feel of her. Filled with wanting.

He wasn't thinking anymore, wasn't asking himself if he'd lost his mind. He might have, but in losing it, he'd found something else.

As the urgency continued to build, he struggled to keep up with it, so that it wouldn't overwhelm him.

Sylvie's breathing was coming in snatches, telling him she was right there with him. She dug her nails into his back as she arched, desperate to achieve that final, fantastic surge.

With one last powerful thrust, Jefferson brought them both to a cresting release. He felt her cry out his name against his mouth and savored the taste of her breath.

And then he held her close to him, because he needed to revel in this moment—when he'd rediscovered himself as a man.

Even as their bodies cooled and their breathing slowed, Jefferson held Sylvie close to him. Feeling her heart beat beside his was somehow comforting.

He'd missed this.

Missed the intimacy, the upward surge, the final, breathtaking moment of mindlessness when the two of them existed as one.

He tried to hang on to that feeling for as long as he possibly could.

CHAPTER ELEVEN

SYLVIE RAISED HER HEAD, her soft, flame-colored hair lightly sweeping across his chest, causing ripples along his skin and widening whirlpools deep inside his belly. Jefferson could feel his gut reflexively tighten against the onslaught, but it was too late. He'd already been captured.

Wow.

That was the only word that Jefferson, eloquent to a fault, could think of to encompass what had just happened here between them. To him.

Wow.

A smile played along his lips as he threaded his fingers through her hair. The sensuous, silky feel of it wove its way through him. Making him want. Again.

He was far from a novice when it came to love-making, but everything about this felt brand new.

Unaware of the effect she was having on him, Sylvie cocked her head, straining to listen. Was that her imagination, or had she just heard a noise coming from the first floor of the gallery?

"What is it?" Jefferson asked, lightly skimming his thumb along her bottom lip.

Sylvie struggled to focus. "Do you hear something?"

Taking her seriously, Jefferson paused for a second, listening. All he heard was her…breathing. He smiled, shaking his head.

Other than the distant murmur of voices from the street, it was as dead as a tomb inside the gallery. Except, Jefferson thought, amending the analogy slightly, he'd never felt so alive. Thanks to her.

"Just the pounding of my heart," he told her.

His answer made her laugh and feel warm inside. It had been a long time since she'd felt that way. A long time. The noise she thought she'd heard was gone, if it had ever existed.

Probably just her imagination, she decided. The same imagination that had felt the earth move a few minutes ago.

"That must be it," she told him as she spread her hand over his chest. She could feel his heart beating beneath her palm. It was a soothing sensation. Sylvie leaned her head on top of her hand, her eyes on his. "They're right," she declared softly, without preamble.

Things were going on inside of him. Things he was trying to recognize, to assess, even as he just wanted to lie there and steep himself in these delicious sensations.

"About?"

"Still waters running deep." *I owe you, Charlotte, Melanie and Renee.* "I would have never thought, looking at you, that…" She didn't finish. She didn't have to. She could tell that he understood her meaning. Smiling, she repeated the sentiment she had uttered earlier this evening. "You are a man of many, many talents, Jefferson Lambert."

And no one was more surprised about some of them than he was, Jefferson thought. He was quite sure tonight had been much more of a revelation to him than it had to her.

Very gently, he brought his hands to Sylvie's sides and moved her so that her body was once more against his, this time fitting neatly on top.

Jefferson saw the spark of pleasure entering her eyes. Less than a second later, he could feel excitement surging through his loins once again. Gathering her even closer, he splayed his hands across her buttocks as he felt himself hardening. She made him feel tireless, young. Eternal.

"Many talents," Sylvie murmured, bringing her mouth down to his.

Within moments, she'd lost herself again in the powerful, vibrant, heretofore undiscovered country that he brought her to. Any thoughts of things that went bump in the night were all forgotten.

AT THE OTHER END of the hotel and two flights up, Luc's heart was pounding wildly in his chest, feeling as if it were going to burst right out at any moment. For a completely different reason.

Leaning against the door, he stared unseeing into the darkness. He didn't bother turning on the small flashlight he'd brought with him earlier. His gloved fingers were locked in a death grip around the small rectangular object he held close. At this moment, he wasn't sure he could release it even if his life depended on it. It was as if his hands had become sealed to the painting, as much a part of it as the frame that surrounded it.

For a moment, all he could hear was the sound of his rapid breathing. It agitated rather than soothed him, but he couldn't seem to slow it down.

Damn, he had no idea how he had managed to get away with this. The odds were astronomically against him, he'd been a fool to chance it. Yet, he'd succeeded. Somehow, he had managed to get into the art gallery—the only easy part of his plan—remove the painting and bring it all the way back up to this room without a single person crossing his path.

Luck, that capricious femme fatale that had eluded his father in his later years, had seen fit to turn her beatific smile on him. She'd been at his side tonight, his only companion on the way from the gallery to this room.

Turning the painting around, Luc stared down at it, trying to adjust his eyes to the faint light coming through the window. But for a moment he couldn't see anything. Lights seemed to be flashing as frantic thoughts assailed him from all directions.

Get a grip, damn it, he ordered himself.

He glanced around the room. A broken pipe had stained the carpet, so the room would be empty until Monday, when the new carpet was installed. But where could he put the painting?

This wasn't right.

Luc felt torn. He wasn't some masked avenger, trying to right a wrong that had been done to his father by some faceless corporation. The Marchands were a family—his father's family. Taking this painting was going to have repercussions. He was hurting people he had come to care about in a short time. People who were his blood. And making them lose the hotel wouldn't bring his father back.

His hands were shaking. Playing hide-and-seek with a priceless piece of art wasn't right. He felt bad just holding the painting. He had to put it back.

Taking a deep breath, Luc slowly opened the door. The sound of voices down the hallway had him shutting it again. His heart slammed against his chest and continued pounding. He'd been lucky so far, but how long would that luck hold out? The surveillance cameras within the gallery and the lobby had been disabled, but the power could come back on at any minute. As he had been taking the painting from the wall, he'd thought he heard a noise coming from the back room. He'd convinced himself it was just his imagination—or his guilty conscience. Now he wasn't so sure.

He had to stay calm. Think clearly. Not take any uncalculated risks. That had been his father's mistake. Being reckless.

His job now was to stash this painting and figure out what to do with it by Monday.

The uneasiness he'd been experiencing all night intensified. Made him nauseated.

SYLVIE SLOWLY OPENED her eyes, a dreamy expression on her face. Small pools of daylight were advancing along the gallery's wooden floors, extending into the small back room through the open door.

Morning.

Oh, God.

Sylvie bolted upright as the realization penetrated the soft fog around her brain. She bumped her head smack into Jefferson's face. His presence next to her registered belatedly.

"Ow!" she cried, rubbing the spot where they'd made hard contact. She looked at him accusingly. "What are you doing?"

If his chin hurt, he gave no indication. "Watching you sleep."

Sylvie stopped rubbing her head and stared at him. "Why?"

He was smiling. "Seemed like the thing to do." Very gently, he ran his knuckles along her cheek. "It's been a long time since I woke up beside someone."

He made her catch her breath. She longed to draw out this moment, to savor it and just lie beside him, talking until they both ran out of things to say. And then maybe make love again. And to savor that, too.

But that was a life that belonged to the carefree woman she had once been, not to the responsible mother who not only had run this art gallery into the black, but was now also thinking about branching out to take over a second gallery, one that wasn't affiliated with the hotel or her family. Something of her own. That woman didn't have time to linger with a brand-new lover, didn't have time to waste on something that had no future.

Even if she ached to do so.

Sylvie reached out and touched his face. She had to go. The hotel would be recovering from whatever ill effects last night's blackout had created. She would be needed, or at the very least missed. She didn't want any search party to encounter her like this.

With effort, Sylvie banked down the sadness that was trying to take hold. "I have a life to get back to."

Turning the hand that was against his cheek, Jefferson pressed a kiss to the center of her palm. He wasn't trying to keep her. He, more than anyone, understood what it was like to have responsibility. It seemed ironic now to be losing what he'd just found because of it.

"Yes, I know."

She felt a very real, very strong shiver up her spine. "You're not helping."

"Sorry." The look in his eyes told her that he really wasn't. Temptation loomed, large and demanding, its fingers reaching for her.

Sylvie dragged a hand through her hair. "What time is it?"

Jefferson glanced at his watch, the only thing that hadn't come off last night. "Almost seven."

That galvanized her. The gallery didn't open until nine, but Charlotte was usually in her office by seven, if she'd even gone home last night. What if she decided to swing by the gallery for a spot check? The last thing Sylvie wanted was to be discovered like this, naked beside an equally naked hotel guest. Never mind that Charlotte had arranged all this. That wouldn't be the part that her sister would remember.

It had been very hard for Sylvie to live down her reputation, to get her family to take her seriously instead of just thinking of her as the wild one, the one who always screwed up. If any of them found out that instead of keeping vigil the way she was supposed to, she had spent the night making love with her "date," she'd spend the rest of her life trying to atone for it.

Shifting off the sofa that had narrowly accommodated them both, she got up and began getting dressed.

Jefferson watched, fascinated. He could feel his body heating all over again. That made—what— three times? Four? He'd never been like this before.

"Need help?" he offered.

She glanced at his face, saw his expression. An image of a fox offering to feed a chicken flashed through her mind. She laughed, shaking her head. "Any help from you would be counterproductive."

"You might have a point," he agreed.

Swiftly, he hurried into his own clothes. Sylvie was already dressed and in the gallery proper as he was slipping on his jacket.

Her cry of alarm had him rushing out to see what had happened.

"What's wrong?" Jefferson quickly scanned the

area for the source of her distress. There was no one else there, and nothing, at first glance, looked to be out of place.

It took Sylvie a second to find her voice. She felt shell-shocked, upset and angry, all at once. "It's missing."

She looked about to fly off in two directions at the same time. He put his hands on her shoulders, holding her in place. "What's missing?" he asked, enunciating slowly.

"The Wyeth." It was almost a sob. How could she have let this happen? *When* had it happened? Oh God, what was her grandmother going to say? What was her *mother* going to say?

"The Wyeth," he repeated.

Sylvie pointed to the back wall.

"My grandmother's…" Her voice trailed off. She tried again. "The Wyeth was on loan from my grandmother, and now…" How could this have happened? And why on her watch, of all things? "And now it's not here. It was here last night, and now…" She struggled not to let panic get the better of her. "That noise," she said suddenly, turning to him, her eyes wide. "That noise I told you that I thought I heard last night…it must have been the thieves."

He wasn't so sure. "The power failure had already hit the hotel by the time you got back here," he reminded her. "Maybe whoever took the painting had already gotten it by then. If that's the case, then it's not your fault."

The old Sylvie would have jumped at the possibility. But she knew that the scenario he'd described was improbable. She thought for a moment, trying hard to remember if the painting had been there when she'd done a cursory check after they'd first walked in. But it had been dark, and all she'd been thinking about was her growing attraction to Jefferson.

"I can't remember if the space was empty or not," she confessed. "I knew the other two paintings on that wall were gone—I loaned them to Maddy. So I didn't pay much attention. I can't say for sure if the Wyeth was there." God did that sound lame, she thought, even to her own ears. What was it going to sound like to Mama and Charlotte?

He hesitated for a moment, then slipped his hand down her back in a gesture of comfort. "Do you want me to call the police?"

Her head jerked up, horror on her face. Police detectives coming into the gallery would do nothing to help the hotel's reputation.

"Oh, God, no." She realized how panicky she sounded and tempered her tone. "At least, not yet. If it turns out to be one of the guests…" Her brain was beginning to hurt. "Maybe something can be worked out. The hotel doesn't need any bad publicity, any kind of notoriety, especially right now."

"What's so different about now?"

Sylvie waved her hand at the question. She'd already said too much to an outsider. "I'd like to keep this quiet for a little while…."

He read between the lines. "By 'quiet,' do you mean you want to keep this from everyone?"

Her eyes met his, and although she had no idea how he knew, she realized that he understood how important this was to her. How important it was to make it right. She pressed her lips together ruefully. "Little Sylvie screws up again."

"We still don't know it was your fault," Jefferson told her. She made him want to do things for her, to make things right. "Want me to nose around a little?" Over the course of his career, he'd picked up some tips from the investigator his firm used. He could put them to use now.

The offer caught her off guard. Sylvie stared at him, bemused despite the gravity of the situation. "You're going to tell me that you're a closet private investigator, as well?"

He was good at looking beyond the obvious, and he was good at blending in and listening. Those might not seem like very sexy or stimulating traits, but they did serve their purpose. "People tend to talk when I'm around," he admitted. "They don't see me as a threat and they don't think I'm paying attention."

Though in a hurry, and feeling the tension building within her, Sylvie still stopped to stare at Jefferson. He made himself sound so bland, so average. Nothing, as far as she was concerned, was further from the truth. He was a distinguished, good-looking man with a brain, who knew how to treat and please a woman. How could he describe himself in terms that made him sound like wallpaper?

"Have people always made a habit of underestimating you like this?"

He liked the way she'd phrased that. Liked, he thought, pretty much everything about her. He knew that whatever was between them didn't have a prayer of going anywhere, but he wanted to help. "I'd better get up to my room and change if I'm going to be any use to you."

"Change," she echoed. Sylvie looked down at what she was wearing. Definitely not daytime wear. That reminded her—she had yet to check in on her daughter. There would be questions to answer, mainly from *Grand-mère*. She braced herself. "Oh, God, me, too."

Even her mother was going to wonder about her being out all night, Jefferson guessed. In the eyes of a parent, a child was always a child, no matter how many candles burned on the birthday cake.

"Relax. You were *supposed* to spend the night in the gallery, remember?"

Her eyes twinkled. "Not the way I spent it," she countered.

He leaned his head closer to hers. "Power was down," Jefferson whispered conspiratorially. "More than likely, the local news stations won't have time to carry the story of what happened in the back room of a hotel gallery."

She laughed and picked up her purse. As she led the way out, her heels clicking on the parquet floor, she could have sworn they kept repeating, *Gone, gone, gone.*

Hopefully, not for long, she prayed, locking the doors. *Locking the barn door after the horses are gone,* she mocked herself. But if there were looters, she didn't want to take any chances on their making a return appearance. The Wyeth had been the most costly item in the gallery, but there were paintings and jewelry from local artists, and their work was important to them.

"I'll call you later," Jefferson promised.

About to hurry down the corridor, Sylvie looked at him quizzically.

"To let you know if I hear anything," he added, gently reminding her of his offer to keep his eyes and ears open about the missing painting. That he wanted to call her because of last night was something he needed to quietly explore himself before he admitted it to her. He doubted that she'd be receptive anyway. Women like Sylvie had to beat men off with a stick.

"Right."

At this moment, Sylvie felt as if there were a thousand random thoughts swimming around in her head at the same time. As soon as she tried to focus on one, something else came flying at her. She needed to get hold of herself, to think clearly about one thing at a time.

She took exactly two steps before she swung around and doubled back. Jefferson stared at her as she grabbed him by the lapels, raised herself up on her toes and kissed him on the mouth, hard.

The next moment, she was off and running again.

Jefferson ran his index finger along his lips. The woman did leave an impression. For a moment, he thought of hurrying after her and walking with her as far as the elevator, but then he decided that maybe Sylvie could use a little time alone to pull herself together.

So could he.

Last night had been a page out of someone else's book, not his. It was more like something Blake would have experienced.

Blake. He realized that he'd lost track of the man. If he knew Blake, his friend had probably made the most of the situation.

Well, hadn't he done the same himself?

And then Jefferson reconsidered. Last night hadn't been about making the most of an unexpected opportunity, it had been about discovering himself. About discovering life. He hadn't felt this alive, this vibrant, this—okay, happy—in years.

And confused. Definitely confused. But when it came to knowing Sylvie Marchand, he had a strong feeling that being confused kind of went with the territory.

CHAPTER TWELVE

"YOU SEEM FLUSTERED, Sylvie," Anne observed, following her daughter into her bedroom. Sylvie had come sailing into her apartment, practically at a dead run, and dashed into the bedroom, saying she had to get back to the hotel as soon as she showered and changed. "Is everything all right at the hotel?"

In the other bedroom, Anne's mother and grand-daughter were still sleeping the sleep of the very young and the very old. Stuck in the middle with more pent-up energy than she was allowed to use these days, Anne had been awake for over an hour, puttering in the kitchen, when she heard the front door open. One look at Sylvie's face and she was concerned. It wasn't often that her daughter appeared so harried.

Anne became more concerned when Sylvie hurried by her, not stopping to give any straight answers to her questions.

Grabbing the first fresh blouse and skirt she came to in her closet, Sylvie paused only long enough at her bureau to pull out a bra and panties, tossing everything on her bed before rushing off to the bathroom.

"As fine as they can be, Mama, given that there was a power failure and everyone gets a little nervous in the dark."

Raised in an unselfconscious atmosphere that Anne had done her best to foster, Sylvie had no qualms about changing in front of her mother. She quickly stripped off her clothing without bothering to close the bathroom door in case there was some other question she needed to answer. Or evade.

The next moment, she was in the shower stall, moving as fast as she could.

Anne frowned to herself, picking up the dress her daughter had hastily discarded. Sylvie was racing around like someone on borrowed time. Something wasn't right. The hotel had had its share of trouble lately. Was this about more of the same?

Taking a large bath towel, she placed it within Sylvie's easy reach on the rack and then paused as a realization struck her.

"Sylvie?"

Sylvie raised her voice to be heard above the running water. "Yes, Mama?"

"Where is your underwear?"

Sylvie felt as if she'd just been struck with a two-by-four across the forehead. For a second, everything froze.

Sylvie closed her eyes. *Her underwear.* She'd been in such a hurry to get back, she must have forgotten her bra and panties at the gallery. But saying that would only lead to more questions. Like, what were they doing off in the first place?

Digging deep, Sylvie managed to retrieve behavior that had been all but forgotten, buried in her long-ago yesterdays.

She brazened it out. "I decided to be daring last night."

"And were you?" Anne finally asked, trying to keep her voice as nonchalant as possible. "Daring," she added when there was no response.

Mothers and daughters shouldn't be having this kind of conversation, Sylvie thought. And then an image of her own daughter flashed in her mind. If Daisy Rose ever tried to shut her out…

As she got out of the shower and quickly toweled herself dry, Sylvie took pity on her mother. Seeing this from the other side really was a bear, she thought. This new perspective created an entire list of things for which she wished she could apologize to her mother.

"The blackout made things difficult for everyone, Mama." It was a nonanswer, but it was the best she could do under the circumstances and not lie. She absolutely hated lying.

Sylvie realized she was getting away with a mild version of the Spanish Inquisition. Had her grandmother been up, as well, the brass knuckles would have come out within seconds of her crossing the threshold. It wouldn't matter that Sylvie didn't want to say anything, didn't want to leave herself open to criticism because of her indiscretion and especially didn't want Celeste to find out about the missing painting. Her grandmother had a way of extracting information no one wanted to volunteer.

Sylvie moved as quickly as she could. The first order of business was to see if any of the surveillance cameras had somehow managed to stay working, despite the power failure. If she had a clue, just one little clue as to who had taken the painting, she was convinced she could get it back. Blessed with a glib tongue, she knew how to swing a deal, whether it was with a patron, a guest, or some opportunist off the street. She would have liked nothing better than have the thief thrown into jail, but that wouldn't solve anything. Patience, bribery and a certain amount of luck were the keys to getting the Wyeth back.

But no police.

"I'll see you later, Mama. I'll call if there's anything to tell." God but she was getting good at double-talk, Sylvie thought. "Thanks for taking care of Daisy Rose for me." Planting a kiss on her mother's cheek, Sylvie took a quick peek at her sleeping daughter, then hurried out of the apartment again, her fresh clothes clinging to her still damp body.

SYLVIE WAS BEYOND BREATHLESS as she hurried back into the hotel, leaving the beleaguered valet to try to figure out just where to park her car this time. The lot the hotel used was filled to capacity.

Crossing the lobby in record time, she nodded at Luc, who was back at his post at the information desk. Although she would have liked to put off telling Charlotte about the stolen painting, she hated having things hang over her head. Now that she had washed the scent of Jefferson's cologne from her skin, she felt a little more capable of facing her sister.

She spotted Charlotte talking to a group of men and women—tourists, she thought by the way they were dressed. They were smiling, so that was a positive sign. This was probably as good a time as any to check in with her sister.

As the group dispersed, Charlotte looked up and saw her. Sylvie felt as if their eyes locked. As she approached, she saw that the expression on her oldest sister's face had turned somber.

Tiny fingers of panic fluttered over her. Had Charlotte heard about the Wyeth? Had she come into the gallery looking for her, and seen the empty spot for herself? Did Charlotte know that in all likelihood, she'd been making love with Jefferson when the painting was taken?

Excuses rose to her lips with lightning speed. Sylvie forced them back. She wasn't going to say anything, wasn't going to take the initiative and tell Charlotte her side of the story. Not yet. She'd learned that it was best to let the other person do the talking. That way she could gauge exactly what Charlotte knew. Or, with luck, didn't know.

"Hello, Charlotte." She did her best to sound breezy, even though she felt anything but. "You look as if you're about to attend a funeral. Your own," she added after a second's pause. She offered Charlotte a thousand-watt smile. "It can't be that bad, really," she declared. "Whatever it is, the hotel will recover." She thought of the damage they'd suffered because of Katrina. "It always has before." It was a sentiment, a phrase, that she intended to keep on repeating in hope that it would eventually calm Charlotte down.

To her surprise, Charlotte wasn't looking at her as if she was horribly disappointed. If Sylvie wasn't mistaken, that was compassion in her sister's eyes. That didn't make any sense.

Sidetracked for a moment by what Sylvie had just said, Charlotte tried to be reassuring. "Some of the guests are complaining that there was minor theft during last night's excitement. I'm going to have Security check them out, separate any real theft from the opportunists trying to cash in on the chaos—"

"Good idea," Sylvie said with a degree of enthusiasm that might have been, in her judgment, just a little over the top. Charlotte was a workaholic, but she wasn't stupid.

"Sylvie…"

Oh, God, here it came. The blame, the recriminations. The disappointment. She couldn't wait for it, couldn't just stand docilely by and allow herself to be drowned in it. "Look, Charlotte, I have an explanation—"

Charlotte blinked, her face a road map of confusion. "What?"

Sylvie suddenly realized that maybe they weren't on the same wavelength. She didn't want to bring her lack of judgment to Charlotte's attention if her sister didn't know anything about it. Pressing her lips together a moment, she stopped her words of defense. "You first."

Charlotte took a deep breath, hating to be the bearer of bad news. "He's here."

Sylvie stared, no more enlightened now than she was a minute ago. "Who's here?"

"Shane." Charlotte said the name as if it burned her tongue. As far as she was concerned, the man who had left her sister to face parenthood alone was worthless scum. Had she known that he was checking into their hotel, she would have told him that his room had been given to someone else. But now her hands were tied. "He's here and he's asking for you."

For a second, Sylvie could only stare at her sister blankly. Then she remembered the phone calls. She should have returned the phone calls. If she had, maybe he wouldn't have come. Oh, God. "Shane?"

Charlotte looked into her eyes as if searching for something. "Daisy Rose's father."

Fatigue and worry had shredded Sylvie's patience. "I *know* who Shane is. I was a little wild back then, Charlotte, but I wasn't out of my head." Damn, what was he doing here? Why now? "Did he say why he's asking for me?"

Before Charlotte could answer her, Sylvie felt herself being grabbed around the waist from behind. The next moment, she was airborne and being spun around.

And then she heard someone ask, "How are you doin', luv?"

Recognition was immediate. The slightly over-powering cologne, the affected British accent that habitually came and went during the course of a sentence. It could only be Shane Alexander, the man who had cast a spell on her for a crazy two months—until she came to her senses.

People were staring at them. Sylvie was about to demand that Shane put her down and explain his sudden reappearance in her life, when she saw Jefferson getting off the elevator and walking into the lobby.

And looking straight at her.

At them.

She couldn't tell what he was thinking, but in his place, she wouldn't have been thinking anything good. Sylvie put her hands on top of Shane's and tried to push them off.

"Put me down, Shane."

Shane laughed. It was a deep, throaty, sexy sound. "Hardest bird to sweep off her feet," he said to Charlotte as he set Sylvie down again.

Sylvie swung around to face him. "I'm not a bird, Shane, I'm a woman. I think that might have been your first mistake." *And mine was in thinking that you could ever build a relationship with anyone but the reflection in your mirror.*

Out of the corner of her eye, she saw that Jefferson had stopped walking her way. She didn't exactly want him in the same area as Shane because she didn't know what the latter was capable of saying, but she didn't want Jefferson going away, either.

The last thing she wanted was for him to think there was something still going on between her and this rock-and-roll has-been.

Mustering the best smile she could, Sylvie beckoned Jefferson over, fervently wishing she'd had more than the space of a faster-than-the-speed-of-light shower to mull over their situation. If they even *had* a situation.

There was a lot to sort through.

Relationships, she thought, never used to be this hard.

Satisfied that Jefferson wasn't about to walk away nursing a wrong impression, Sylvie turned to really take a look at Shane for the first time in three years.

He'd aged, she realized. More than just a little. More than three years' worth. He still wore his hair long—it was past his shoulders—but there were streaks of gray in it now. He looked like a mountain man who had lost his way. The hard living he'd subjected his body to throughout the years was all there in his face. He looked like thirty miles of bad road.

He sure wasn't pretty anymore, Sylvie thought, almost feeling sad for Shane. She wondered if he still had his voice, or if that, too, had suffered the ravages of his lifestyle.

"What brings you here?" she asked, her tone just shy of curt. "Touring with the band?" If Lynx had gotten back together and was providing Mardi Gras entertainment anywhere in New Orleans, she hadn't heard of it. Glancing at Charlotte, she saw her sister shake her head.

"If you'd answered your phone, you'd know why I'm here." Draping one long arm around her shoulders, Shane laughed harshly. "The band and I are history, luv. They had too much ego. I'm looking to start my own band. I was carrying them, anyway."

If anyone in the band had had too much ego it had been Shane, she thought.

"Well, good luck with that," she said, cutting him off before he could launch into a lengthy discussion about his fights with the band or his plans for a new group. She had all the crises she felt capable of handling right now. Listening to Shane go on and on was something she didn't have the stomach or the time for.

Sylvie began to move away, but Shane caught hold of her wrist, stopping her.

She saw Jefferson step forward, his shoulders squared. *Like a big protector.* Arthur, about to banish a renegade Lancelot. The image made her smile. And though she wouldn't have thought it was her style, the image also warmed her.

Shane had both age and weight in his favor, but of the two, Jefferson looked more fit. In a contest, he could probably hold his own, if not take Shane. Even so, it wasn't something she wanted to see happen. She'd grown up, Sylvie realized. She didn't want to witness an exchange of blows or even heated words on her behalf.

Sylvie could tell by Shane's stance that he was

feeling territorial. Because she didn't want him to think there was a chance in hell he could just pick up where they'd left off before Daisy Rose, Sylvie turned and brushed her lips against Jefferson's cheek.

She managed to surprise not only Jefferson and Shane, but Charlotte, as well.

"Hi, honey," she said cheerfully to Jefferson. "Getting impatient?"

SYLVIE HAD CAUGHT him up short. Jefferson was still scrutinizing the somewhat eccentric-looking man in front of her. He was vaguely aware that the woman she'd introduced last night as her sister was now looking at him in the same way: as if she was weighing and measuring him.

Not altogether certain exactly what Sylvie needed of him, only that he wanted to be able to provide it, he responded, "Something like that."

Shane looked temporarily confused, as if he wasn't quite sure if he'd been insulted. The next moment, he leered at Sylvie, then cast a condescending glance toward the man she'd just greeted. "She's a pistol, that one, isn't she?"

Jefferson took an instant dislike to the man. He vaguely recognized him from a poster Emily had had on her wall advertising a Lynx tour. So, this was the father of Sylvie's child. What the hell had Sylvie been thinking?

And what the hell was *he* thinking, having feelings for her?

He reined himself in. He was getting carried away again, something he wasn't accustomed to. There was no accounting for taste, and he knew that rock stars held a certain allure for young women. He hoped to God his Emily would have more sense.

"Where I come from," he informed Shane evenly, barely containing his contempt, "we don't discuss women as if they were inanimate objects."

Sylvie's eyes widened. Jefferson was defending her honor. Like some Southern aristocrat from a different era. She felt like throwing her arms around Jefferson's neck.

Shane's eyes became two dark slits as he regarded the other man. "I don't know where you're from, bloke, but from where I'm standing, I'd say they've got sticks up their butts there."

This was going to escalate, Sylvie realized. Jefferson wasn't about to back down and Shane didn't have enough brains to back off.

She quickly moved between the two men, standing closer to Jefferson, her body language telling Shane just who she was siding with.

"This stops here, Shane," she ordered. "You should have let me know you were coming. This is our busy season. I don't have any time to catch up." She was about to say that he might as well go, when he threw a grenade into her garden.

"I tried to let you know, but you never answered your damn messages. Besides, I'm not here to catch up, luv," he told her. "I'm here about Daisy Rose."

Maternal instincts had her stiffening like a road

warrior, ready to do battle at a moment's notice. "What *about* Daisy Rose?" she said tersely.

"I want her."

The words were simple, but she found she couldn't process his statement and make any sense of it. "What?"

"I want her," Shane repeated. He wasn't accustomed to having to explain himself. His was a world where he expressed a desire and it was met. Frowning, he tried again. "Look, I'm getting married next month."

The news hit Sylvie like a blow to the stomach. When they'd been together, Shane had sworn six ways from sundown that he was never going to get tied down to any one woman, adding that if he ever did, it would be her. She'd been flattered by the line, had actually believed it. Now she knew he'd said it to break down any defenses she might have had.

He'd obviously played her for a fool, and it stung, even as she strove to show him that it didn't.

"Congratulations," she said icily.

"Yeah, thanks." Shane didn't seem to notice that the sentiment wasn't tendered with any warmth. "Patty wants kids," he told her.

Patty. That would be his bride-to-be, she surmised.

"So why don't you have one together?" Jefferson inquired mildly.

Shane scowled at the interruption. "Who the hell is this bloke?"

Exasperated, Sylvie struggled not to lose her

temper. Since last night, it had been just one thing after another. She wasn't sure how much more she could take.

"Damn it, Shane, will you stop with the accent? Everyone knows you're from New York. And as for who this is—" she hooked her arms through Jefferson's "—this is Jefferson Lambert. My fiancé."

She slanted a glance toward Jefferson and was grateful to see that he took in stride the bombshell she'd just dropped on him. No surprise was evident in his expression. He hadn't so much as winced. The man was one cool customer. Thank God.

Charlotte's jaw, however, had dropped about as low as it physically could go. And she was staring at Sylvie with huge, disbelieving eyes.

"Sylvie," Charlotte cried.

"I'll talk to you later, Charlotte," Sylvie told her in measured tones. She turned to Shane, trying to contain her anger. "I don't know what's running through your head about Daisy Rose, but you can't have her. You can't just walk into her life after three years—after never even seeing her once—and suddenly want to play daddy."

Sylvie knew that Shane had never let logic deter him. Now was no exception.

"She's half mine."

"She's not a piece of cake to be divided up equally," Sylvie shot back. "You gave up rights to her, remember? I believe your exact words were, 'Good luck, luv' as you walked away. When I called you after she was born to tell you that you had a healthy daughter, you mumbled something like 'huh,' and hung up."

He looked annoyed that she would bring any of that up. "I was younger then."

Sylvie rolled her eyes. "You were forty. That's not exactly a kid."

Obviously changing tack, he lowered his voice and smiled at her as if she were a nubile fan he'd selected to seduce for the evening.

"Give me a break, Sylvie. Don't say no." He ran his hand up along her arm. "Patty would make a great mother."

She pulled back as she regarded him coldly. "So make her one."

He sighed, exasperated. "She doesn't want to get pregnant. Too messy."

Shane had finally met his match, she thought. Someone as acutely narcissistic as he was. "Sounds like a winner already. I can see why you're in love."

Angry at the hoops Sylvie was making him jump through, he glared at her. "You always were a ball buster."

"Apologize," Jefferson ordered evenly. His voice was low but there was no mistaking his intention to back up his command if need be.

Shane tossed his head, his hair flying over his shoulder, nostrils flaring.

Alarmed, Sylvie tried to draw Jefferson away. She couldn't budge him. "Jefferson, really, it's okay."

"No," he replied, his eyes never leaving the tall, thin guitarist, "it's not. Apologize."

CHAPTER THIRTEEN

VOICES OF HOTEL GUESTS in the lobby faded into the background as the two men stood toe to toe before the front desk.

It was a well-known fact that Shane Alexander was not accustomed to hearing the word *no*. He'd spent almost two decades having his every whim attended to. But, in the end, Shane's sense of survival prevailed over his inflated ego and he grudgingly spat out the required words that would bring an end to this standoff.

Without looking at Jefferson, Shane mumbled, "Didn't mean anything by it, luv. You know that. Just me talkin'." His mouth curved as he inevitably made another stab at seducing her. One side of his mouth lifted. "You and me did a lot of talkin' once."

Sylvie knew that look. Shane wasn't referring to any verbal language. The "talking" he was reminiscing about had taken place beneath the sheets. A million years ago, in another lifetime….

"Once," she agreed, her tone dismissive, telling him that all that belonged buried in the past. A past she did not want to revisit. She nodded toward the elevator bank. "Don't you have a would-be future wife to see to?"

Temper flared in his eyes. Shane didn't like being dismissed. But because of the man standing beside Sylvie like some kind of medieval gatekeeper, he retreated. For the time being.

His parting words did not reassure her. "I'm not giving up, you know, luv. There're a lot of ways to skin a cat."

Jefferson wasn't completely sure what was going on here, or just what Sylvie and Shane's history entailed beyond the daughter she obviously adored, but he did know when someone was being threatened. He looked at the aging rocker coldly.

"But then all you have is a mess on your hands," he said to Shane pointedly.

There was barely suppressed fury in Shane's eyes. He shoved his hands into the back pockets of his artistically torn jeans. "Ain't over yet," he promised again with no trace of what he viewed as his trademark accent. And he stormed off.

Charlotte released the breath she'd been holding. When she looked at Sylvie, her eyes were filled with concern. "That jackass doesn't really stand a chance, does he? He can't take our Daisy Rose, can he?"

Just one damn thing after another. This newest disaster had Sylvie so furious she could hardly form coherent sentences. She hung on to the anger. It helped blot out the vein of fear that ran through it.

"So that the bimbo he's marrying can play with a life-size baby doll?" she snapped. "Over my dead body." Her mind scrambled for an immediate solution that didn't involve buying a box of ammunition. "I'll go into the Witness Protection Program with her first."

In the face of fear, there was an increased need for logic, Jefferson knew. Very gently, he pointed out, "You won't be put into Witness Protection just because you don't want your child's father to have joint custody."

Joint custody was bad enough, but Sylvie had a feeling that Shane was talking about full custody. She knew how his mind worked. Thank God she'd come back here to her family, to a stable life. Two years ago, despite the fact that he had once been part of a rock band that had less than a stellar reputation, he probably would have had more financial security to offer Daisy Rose. At least on paper. Given the right judge, things might have gone Shane's way.

She clenched her hands at her sides. Shane was *never* going to get custody of Daisy Rose, not as long as there was breath in her body.

"Then I'll have to come up with something they'll want to protect me for, won't I," she replied, her voice low, steely and determined.

Taking one of her hands in his, Jefferson moved his fingers in between hers and unclenched her fist. His tone was soothing. "You will," he assured her, then amended, "We will." He wasn't sure just where that had come from. He only knew that he meant it. Meant to protect her and the child she loved.

How did he know? she wondered. How could he

look at her and say that with such confidence? Was he just humoring her? But even as the questions seemed to bounce around in her brain, she could feel herself calming down. It was going to be all right. She could handle this—

"Mama! Mama!"

Sylvie stiffened as she heard the cry. Daisy Rose? Startled, she turned in the direction of her daughter's voice. She was just in time to see a child hurtling toward her. In less than a heartbeat, Daisy Rose had wrapped her little arms as far around her mother's thighs as she could manage.

Stunned, grateful that Shane had left, Sylvie ran her hand over the little girl's curly hair. "What are you doing here, sugar?"

"Hugging you," Daisy Rose told her simply, her voice muffled.

Sylvie could feel her daughter's warm breath against her legs, right through her skirt.

"She wanted to see you," Anne told her, coming up behind the girl. Daisy Rose had bolted from her the moment she'd seen her mother. The little girl's legs moved a great deal faster than Anne's did these days.

But much as she loved her daughter, she didn't have time for Daisy Rose right now. She needed to track down the missing painting, Sylvie thought. Though, Shane's threat had her holding onto her little girl tightly.

"Mama, you're squishing me," Daisy Rose protested.

"Sorry."

"Daisy Rose really wanted to see you," Anne said.

Sylvie looked at the small, round face that was regarding her so intently. "I've got a lot to do today, cupcake—"

"Not the least of which is to give me details," Charlotte interjected, as if suddenly coming to.

"Details?" Sylvie prayed that Charlotte was not referring to the missing Wyeth. Wouldn't she have said something immediately if she knew that it had been taken?

Guilt pricked at her. She shouldn't be playing these games. She should have told Charlotte the second she saw that it was missing.

But she did so like this newfound respect that her sister accorded her. If Charlotte knew that she'd spent the night acquainting herself with Jefferson's anatomy and vice versa while someone was making off with the Wyeth, there was no way she would be able to redeem herself, not for the next twenty years.

"Don't give me that," Charlotte scoffed, and looked pointedly at the man whose arm Sylvie had just been hanging on to. The man who looked as if he'd been prepared to fight for her honor when that loudmouth jerk threw a slur her way. After all the losers who had passed in and out of Sylvie's life, it looked as if she had finally wound up with Clark Kent *and* Superman, rolled into one.

Since it had been her doing, along with Melanie's and Renee's, that had gotten Sylvie and this modern-day white knight together, Charlotte couldn't help wondering if she should feel pleased with herself—or worried as hell. After all, Sylvie had just indicated they were going to get married!

Shifting gears, Charlotte looked at Jefferson. "Are you really her fiancé?"

At any other time, Sylvie might have indulged herself and continued to pull Charlotte's leg just for the fun of it at least for a little while. But she *had* to find that missing painting. Her grandmother would never forgive her carelessness. Yes, the Wyeth was insured, but no one could put a dollar value on a masterpiece—not to mention that the hotel's reputation would be forever damaged. She could just hear it now: "Come to the Hotel Marchand—but watch out for thieves!"

"Sylvie?" Her mother looked at her quizzically.

She waved away the concern of both women. "Of course not. I just said that so Shane would think he's up against more than just a 'mere woman,' which is the way that jackass thinks." She flashed Jefferson a grateful smile. "Thanks for playing along."

A wishful expression flickered over his features. "Does this mean the engagement is over?"

Damn, Sylvie thought, he just kept getting sexier looking all the time. She grinned at him. "'Fraid so."

"Shane?" Anne repeated, both stunned and horrified. "You mean that—" moving so that she was standing behind Daisy Rose, Anne covered her granddaughter's ears and lowered her voice "—that no-good snake-in-the-grass, her father?" When Sylvie nodded, Anne demanded, "What's he doing here?"

Sylvie would have preferred having this discussion somewhere more private, but her mother didn't appear to want to wait for an answer. "He came to ask for custody."

Anne looked as if she had just been physically threatened. Instinct had her placing a protective hand on Daisy Rose's shoulder. "Custody?" she echoed.

Sylvie nodded. Daisy Rose gave no indication that she knew the importance of what was being said. "He's getting married and his new wife wants to play house, with all the trimmings."

Anne blew out a breath. As far back as the girls could remember, she had never shouted, never raised her voice or lost her temper. But there was fury in her eyes as she said, "That man is the worst kind of useless vermin."

"Mama," Charlotte cried, stunned.

"Well, he *is,*" Anne said matter-of-factly. "Now, if you're fine with Daisy Rose, Sylvie, I'm meeting someone for brunch."

"Someone?" Sylvie asked, her eyebrows rising.

Anne's cheeks pinkened slightly, but she gave no further details as she kissed her granddaughter goodbye.

Sylvie watched her mother leave. "You know, the best thing that could happen to mother would be to have a man in her life again."

"What!" Charlotte looked appalled.

"A man," Sylvie repeated. "Mama deserves some happiness and there's nothing like the right man to put the curl back in your hair. According to *Grand-mère,* she's been going on morning dog walks with *Grand-mère's* neighbor, William Armstrong, and—"

Sylvie caught her bottom lip between her teeth. This was not a conversation she and her sister needed to have now.

Changing gears, she glanced down at her little handful-and-a-half. "So, munchkin, you missed me?"

"Uh-huh." Always curious, Daisy Rose stared up at the man beside her mother, interest blossoming on her small face. "Who are you?"

Jefferson glanced at Sylvie before answering. Who was he? he wondered. Up until last night, he had thought he knew. But last night had turned everything on its ear. Shaken everything up. Made him want things he'd thought he was beyond.

"That," he said to Daisy Rose with a wink, "is the sixty-four-thousand-dollar question."

Like most only children, Daisy Rose was smart for her age. Everyone at the hotel wanted to teach her something, and her language skills and grasp of numbers were far more advanced than those of most children her age. But this was a larger number than she'd ever tackled before. "Is that more than a gazillion?"

Jefferson pretended to think the question over.

"No, I believe a gazillion beats out sixty-four thousand pretty easily." His answer earned him a huge grin not only from Daisy Rose, but from her mother.

Nothing touched Sylvie faster than someone being nice to her child. "You know child-speak."

He was a single parent who dearly loved his daughter. Who had treated her, from the first, as an adult in the making, even as he savored every moment of her childhood. "I used to be very versed in it when Emily was a little girl."

Sylvie's stomach growled, reminding her that she hadn't had anything to eat since the sandwich at her impromptu picnic dinner. The pie must still be on the tray in her office. She wasn't going to be able to search for the painting with Daisy Rose, anyway, and her daughter loved to eat out. It made her feel like a grown-up.

"Are you up for some breakfast?" she asked Jefferson, then turned to Charlotte. "Is the kitchen back in gear?"

Charlotte nodded. "The staff practically worked overnight, but they've managed to get everything back in order. Speaking of which, I've got to check with Robert about dinner." With a wave, she left the three of them in the lobby.

"If you're real good," Daisy Rose informed Jefferson solemnly, as if imparting a great secret, "the chef makes the pancakes look like Mickey Mouse."

"Then I guess I'll have to be real good," he told her.

Daisy Rose beamed.

Sylvie approved of his answer. And of him. She watched her daughter slip her hand into Jefferson's. Daisy Rose was a friendly child, but she gave her affection cautiously. Yet it was there, in her smile, as she looked up at Jefferson.

Uncertainty nibbled away at her. Should she be running for the hills, or enjoying this? Jefferson seemed like a decent, wonderful man who liked children, but she'd known him less than twenty-four hours. She had to be careful about leading with her emotions instead of her head. She'd done that too often in the past and it had always gotten her into trouble.

Right now, she wished that Charlotte, Melanie and Renee had minded their own business. Then maybe the painting wouldn't be missing and she wouldn't be tied up in indecisive knots.

Daisy Rose was staring at her impatiently. "C'mon, Mama, before they're all gone."

"Yeah, c'mon, Mama," Jefferson laughed.

With a surrendering shrug, Sylvie fell into place on the other side of her daughter. "Let's go."

God but this felt good, he thought. It was so easy to slip back into a role he'd occupied happily when Emily was a girl and Donna was alive.

Part of him was sending out warning flares, telling him to back off now, while he still could. But another part knew that it was already too late. He might as well make the most of this while it lasted.

SOMETHING WAS WRONG.

Frowning, Emily Lambert closed her cell phone again, worried. That made ten times she'd tried to reach her father. Ten times that she'd found herself listening to his recorded voice, telling her to leave a message at the tone.

"I have," she told the phone accusingly. "But you're not returning any of them."

Frustrated, she'd called Blake earlier today. Reaching him hadn't been easy, but she'd succeeded. Not that it had done her any good. Her godfather had told her that he and her father had gotten separated because of the freak blackout that had hit parts of New Orleans. The blackout was the reason she'd begun calling in the first place. The TV had been on last night while she was finishing up her homework and she'd heard the news bulletin. Worried, she'd tried to call her father. And had gotten his voice mail.

Why wasn't he answering his messages? A blackout wouldn't have affected her ability to get through to him. Telephones and cells didn't use electricity. But when she'd called his room last night, there had been no answer. She assumed it was because he wasn't there. But he hadn't picked up first thing in the morning, either.

Something wasn't adding up. Her father was the most dependable person on the face of the earth. Why wasn't he checking his messages?

Emily had the uneasy feeling that her father needed her. He was brilliant at what he did, but he didn't fare all that well on his own away from home, she thought, shaking her head.

Trying to call her father between classes today just wasn't going to cut it. She would only become more and more frustrated. What she needed to do was be there. She made up her mind so fast her brain almost had whiplash, but she knew exactly what she had to do. She had to ditch her classes for the day and fly down to New Orleans. She knew exactly where he was staying. She'd been the one to help make the online reservation.

Reaching into her back pocket, she took out her wallet. She flipped it open and looked inside. The credit card her father had given her for emergencies was right where she had left it. So far, she'd only used it to pay for small items, like books she needed for school or a pair of jeans. Although neither constituted an emergency, the purchases had been okayed by her dad.

This, however, was something completely different. A missing father really was a bone fide emergency.

Emptying her backpack onto the bed, she dumped out her books and hastily threw in a change of clothing and a few necessities. She zipped the backpack up again and gave it a once-over. It looked as if it were still packed with books. Good.

"Bye, Grandma, I'm leaving," she called out cheerfully a few minutes later as she headed out the door. "Gotta dash or I'll be late for the bus."

"Have a good day, Emily," her grandmother called.

Emily felt guilty about lying. But she knew she would feel worse about not doing anything if it turned out something *had* happened to her father. As she hurried away from the house and down the block to the bus stop, she tried her father on her cell one last time. Still no response.

Because she believed in covering all bases and was an optimist at heart, Emily redialed her godfather.

"Talk to me," he said when he answered the phone.

At least she had gotten through to someone. "Uncle Blake, where is he?"

"Emily. Hi." He sounded surprised. "Your dad? He's enjoying himself I guess. The last I saw, he was driving off into the night in a horse-drawn carriage with Sylvie Marchand, the date we hooked him up with. She seems to like him."

"Thanks, Uncle Blake, I gotta go. My bus is here. Bye." She closed the cell before he could say anything. She deliberately didn't tell him about her plans, because, after all, Uncle Blake was an adult and he'd probably try to talk her out of it.

There was no way that was going to happen. Her father driving a carriage? From the sound of it, he might be getting serious about this woman. Why else would he do something so out of character? She frowned. She'd just wanted him to have a little fun, to get back into dating, maybe eventually start seeing someone on a regular basis. But this was happening much too fast. God only knows what he was doing right now.

The bus arrived and Emily boarded it quickly. A sense of urgency was compelling her. She needed to reach her father before he did something they were both going to regret.

Taking a seat, Emily sighed. It was obvious to her that she wasn't through raising him yet.

CHAPTER FOURTEEN

SYLVIE FELT as if her head were splitting. How could so much go wrong in such a short period of time?

A day ago, her biggest concern had been choosing which paintings she was going to lend Maddy. At least those, mercifully, were still where they were supposed to be. She'd verified that nothing had happened to them with a quick call to her friend a few minutes ago. Maddy had assured her the paintings were fine and that she would be sending them back before the afternoon was over.

But now she suddenly found herself having to deal with the theft of an exceedingly expensive painting on one front and a potential custody battle on the other. And that didn't even begin to take in wrestling with her conscience because of what had happened with her "blind" date.

She might have the soul of a neo-flower child, but she'd never been careless about who she slept with. Even at the height of her free-spirit period, she had been monogamous in her relationships. Once she became a mother, that was her most important job, and her most important relationship was with her child.

Granted, the earth had moved for her last night, but that could have been for so many reasons. A long spell of celibacy could have colored her perception of events and her reactions. The bottom line was, there was no possibility of a future for her with a lawyer who hailed from the New England area.

What in God's name could she have been thinking, making love with him?

She turned toward Jefferson abruptly. They were in the restaurant, and although it was way past breakfast time, the chef had made Mickey Mouse pancakes to please Daisy Rose, who was at present happily divesting Mickey of one of his ears.

The little girl was sitting between them. When they had taken their seats, the thought of how idyllic this scene was had flashed through Sylvie's mind. This was the way she would have liked things to be. For Daisy Rose to have a father, a real father. Someone who would also be there for her, not so much to slay dragons as to tell her that the dragons didn't matter. That all that mattered was love.

But that was as much a fantasy as dragons were and she had to stop thinking that way. She needed to have her feet planted squarely on the ground and get her head out of the clouds. Starting now.

"This isn't going to work," she told Jefferson without preamble.

Jefferson raised his eyes to hers. He had just picked up the creamer and was about to pour. "The creamer?" He tipped it. Cream swirled into his coffee. "Seems to work just fine."

"No, not the creamer," she said impatiently, keeping her voice down. Wishing she could keep her feelings in check as easily. "This," she hissed, waving a hand to include the two of them.

Jefferson did not respond immediately. He'd always been fairly good at reading people. And they'd made a connection last night, he and Sylvie, one that transcended the physical. A connection that he never thought he'd make again. It enabled him to read between the lines.

She was afraid, he realized. Bohemian, gypsy-like, a free spirit by every possible definition, Sylvie was still afraid. Afraid of what had happened between them. Of what it meant. And he, the man whose daughter had accused him more than once of wearing both a belt and suspenders when it came to life, wasn't. He wasn't afraid. A little stunned, maybe, but more than willing to take the next step. And the next. To see where this was going.

And to hope.

"Us," Sylvie explained, bordering on exasperation when he said nothing, when he just kept looking at her with those large, calm eyes of his.

"How do you know?" he asked mildly. "You haven't given it much of a chance to survive. Why don't you just watch and see what happens?" he suggested.

She could feel his voice undulating under her skin, could feel herself weakening when she was used to being so strong. It made her feel vulnerable, a state she had vowed never to be in again. "I've got too much to deal with, too much to handle."

He wondered if she saw herself that way, as an isolated entity. "You don't have to do it alone, you know."

"She's not alone," Daisy Rose piped up, a tiny stream of honey trickling down her chin. "Mama has me."

Sylvie could feel tears welling up inside of her, coming from nowhere, threatening to spill out. Oh God, she was falling apart, she thought, trying to quell the onslaught of panic. What was wrong with her? She was acting as if she'd never made love before.

"Yes, I do, baby," she whispered to the child. Raising her eyes to Jefferson, she bit back a plea for help. "I'm coming apart."

"You're not coming apart, Sylvie." There was nothing but sympathy in his eyes as he reached for her hand. "You're having an anxiety attack."

She tried to pull her hand back, but he held it fast. "No, I'm not."

"Yes, you are," he countered firmly. "Nothing to be ashamed of. It can happen to anyone. Your system's on overload and you're panicking. Just remember, no matter how bad it feels, it'll pass." He smiled at her, releasing her hand. "That should help."

She tossed her head. Out of the corner of her eye, she saw Daisy Rose mimicking her.

MARIE FERRARELLA213

"What would you know about panic attacks?" It wasn't a question, it was an accusation.

Another man might have hedged, but Jefferson saw no reason not to tell her the truth. "I had one three weeks after my wife died. I was sure I couldn't make it without her. And damn sure I couldn't handle being a single parent to an eight-year-old." He smiled, thinking how much harder losing Donna would have been if he hadn't had Emily to care for. "Emily's sixteen now. Still alive. And she's turned out pretty well."

Holding her fork in her hand like a scepter, Daisy Rose paused in her final assault on her pancake, which no longer resembled Mickey in the least. She looked up at Jefferson. "Is Emily your little girl?"

"Yes, she is." This one was a sponge, he thought. Very much like his Emily had been. "Would you like to see what she looks like?" When Daisy Rose enthusiastically bobbed her head up and down, Jefferson took his wallet from his pocket and opened it before the little girl. "There." He pointed to a recent photograph he'd just put in last week. "That's Emily."

Taking the wallet into her hands, the three-year-old studied the photograph, then looked up. Very solemnly, she handed the wallet back to him. "She looks like that girl," she declared, pointing a slender finger toward the entrance of the restaurant.

To be polite, Jefferson humored her and turned in his seat to look.

Following the direction that Dairy Rose pointed, he found himself staring at a young woman who looked exactly like his daughter. Who dressed exactly like his daughter.

But he had left Emily back in Boston, his mind insisted. He must be looking at a carbon copy.

STANDING IN THE DOORWAY, Emily scanned the interior of the restaurant slowly, checking the occupants scattered throughout. The desk clerk had told her this was where her father had gone. It was close to two o'clock and most of the lunch crowd had departed, but more than a few couples lingered.

And then she saw him. He was with a woman and a little girl. Waving, Emily hurried over.

"Dad!" she cried. Her father had just enough time to stand up before she launched herself into his arms, backpack and all. "Dad, you're all right."

"Of course I'm all right." Releasing Emily, he tried to make sense of the situation. "Why wouldn't I be? What are you doing here? Don't you have classes?" He looked behind her, half expecting to see his mother-in-law in Emily's wake, but there was only a waitress passing by, bringing someone a huge dessert. "Is your grandmother with you?" Independent though Emily was, he still wouldn't have thought she would just hop on a flight for New Orleans by herself.

After pausing for just a second, Emily tried to answer the questions in the order received. "Looking for you. Yes, but they don't matter, and no, she's not." Satisfied that she had covered everything, she had one crucial question of her own. "Why aren't you answering your cell phone?"

He looked at her blankly. "My cell?"

"Yes." Emily saw the little girl looking up at her, and she smiled at her before reading her father an abbreviated form of the riot act. Now she knew how *he* felt when *she* didn't call in, but that was an observation to save for another time, when she might need it. "I've been calling since last night. There was this story on the news that half of New Orleans was engulfed in some kind of massive power failure." She lowered her voice dramatically. "One of the reporters suggested it might even have been another terror attack." Her eyes narrowed as she fixed him with an accusing look. "And you weren't answering your phone."

Three pairs of female eyes were on Jefferson as he took his cell phone out and examined it. The light was lit. He held it up for Emily to see.

"It's on," he protested.

Emily knew better. "Give me that," she huffed. Taking the phone from him, she pressed a few buttons to scroll through a menu as she checked out her suspicions.

She rolled her eyes. "You have it set on vibrate, not ring," she accused.

Jefferson looked at the silver object, mystified. He had no idea when that had occurred, only that he hadn't been the one to do it—at least, not on purpose. Gadgets were definitely not his thing.

"Must have happened the last call I made," he speculated. "I must have accidentally hit something."

Pressing a few buttons, she returned the phone to its normal mode. A ring echoed before she flipped the phone closed and held it out to him.

"So you're okay." It was more of a statement than a question.

Where he came from, parents worried about kids, not the other way around. And it wasn't as if he hadn't called her when he landed. They'd even talked early last night. Emily worrying about him had been the furthest thing from his mind.

"Why shouldn't I be?"

"I'm Daisy Rose," Daisy Rose announced, tugging on Emily's backpack. She must have felt that she had been patient enough during this exchange. When Emily looked at her, she said, "You're pretty."

Surprised by the compliment, Emily took a second to get her bearings. And then she grinned. "You're pretty, too."

"I know," Daisy Rose replied with confidence. "That's my mama." She pointed to Sylvie. "Her name's Sylvie." With a guileless look, she went on to ask, "Are you going to be my big sister?"

Jefferson had just taken a sip of coffee, and barely managed to swallow as Daisy Rose's question to his daughter blindsided him. He was only grateful that he hadn't spit the liquid out.

Taking a breath to steady himself, he looked at Daisy Rose in disbelief. He hadn't thought the little girl was listening to anything being said around her. Obviously, he'd been wrong. She'd picked up a great deal and had interpreted the information in her own way.

Emily looked at her father, waiting for some kind of denial. Afraid that he might be on the verge of choking, she pounded him on the back until he held up a hand to make her stop.

"Dad?"

"I'm okay," he told her hoarsely. "Although I might need a new back." Before anything else, introductions were in order, he thought. "Emily, this is Sylvie Marchand and her daughter, Daisy Rose. Ladies, this is my daughter, Emily, doing her best imitation of Nancy Drew."

"I was worried," she reminded him.

"You could have called the hotel front desk, or better yet, Blake."

"I did call Uncle Blake." She slanted a look at Sylvie. "He said he thought you were getting serious."

He saw another flash of panic in Sylvie's eyes. Damn Blake, anyway. He always did move his mouth before his mind was engaged.

"No decisions about anything have been made yet," he told her, then looked at Daisy Rose. "And that goes for your question, as well. I promise, you two will be the first to know."

"Oh." He couldn't tell if Emily was relieved, or disappointed.

"Oh," Daisy Rose echoed, imitating Emily. It was clear by the expression on her small face that she'd instantly taken to Emily and had appointed her a role model.

Jefferson probably wanted some time alone with

his daughter, Sylvie thought. Seeing the girl, seeing how old she was, reinforced her conviction that this attraction she felt for Jefferson didn't have a prayer of going anywhere. The sooner she backed away, the sooner she could turn her attention to everything else.

She glanced down at her daughter. "Daisy Rose, honey, I think—"

But Sylvie had no opportunity to finish what she was about to say. From out of nowhere, Shane materialized, bringing with him a woman who looked to be only a few years older than Jefferson's daughter.

She couldn't have been more than twenty-two, Sylvie thought. Obviously, Shane was trying to hang on to a youthful image. There was no way he was going to bring her daughter into this.

"Hello, luv, told you I'd be back," he announced. His attempt to brush a kiss against her cheek had him kissing air instead. At the same time, Sylvie clamped her hand on the only remaining chair at the table, offering it to Emily.

Unfazed, Shane grabbed a chair from another table and dragged it over. Straddling it, he looked directly at Daisy Rose, unmindful that he had left his fiancée standing behind him.

Jefferson rose and offered the young woman his chair. It earned him a small smile that was tinged with embarrassment. It was obvious that Shane's fiancée wasn't accustomed to being slighted. Jefferson retrieved one more chair for himself. The small, round table was becoming very crowded.

Sylvie glanced toward Jefferson as he sat down, her eyes silently begging him not to leave. He had no intention of going anywhere. Especially not when his own daughter was looking at the former rock musician as if he were the Second Coming.

For now, though, Shane's attention was on the smallest member of their table. "Know who I am, luv?" he asked Daisy Rose.

Sylvie was about to say that if his brain had not eroded from all the drinking he'd done, he would remember that she'd written him about that. She'd told Daisy Rose as much as she felt a three-year-old could understand about her father. She'd shown her photographs, not to establish a beachhead for Shane, but to let the little girl know that, like everyone else, she had both a mother and a father.

"You're Shane Alexander—" Emily's voice cracked.

For the first time, she looked her age, Jefferson thought. She was suddenly a love-struck adolescent. Why had she picked this, of all times, to be a typical teenager, he wondered, frustrated. The man was only a little removed from pond scum.

In the face of Emily's adulation, Shane seemed to blossom. "Right you are, luv. Shane Alexander, at your service. Are you a fan?"

"I'm probably your biggest fan," Emily told him with enthusiasm.

The look on Shane's face was almost a leer. "I've always loved my fans."

"That was always part of your trouble," Sylvie

commented. And it was also the reason that they had broken up. Her eye caught Patty's and she could see that the other woman was having the same thoughts. And that she was growing annoyed.

Good for you, Sylvie thought. *Run while you have the chance.*

Shane was pouring on the charm, something he was very good at. "Maybe you'd like to drop by my suite later and I could play something for you."

Emily looked as if she was hardly breathing. "I'd love it."

"No, you wouldn't," Jefferson told her in no uncertain terms.

Emily looked at him the way daughters have been looking at interfering fathers since the beginning of time. "Dad!"

If it was a choice between being Emily's friend and being her father, the role of father won hands down. It was his job to protect her. Especially from predators.

"She's underage," he informed Shane tersely. "And you, I hear, are engaged."

Patty sniffed. "Not if he keeps acting like this." Her carefully made-up eyes narrowed at Shane. She'd obviously exhausted her supply of patience. "Look, why don't you just take your daughter so we can go back to L.A.?"

Shane held up a hand to silence Patty. "Would you like that, honey?" he asked Daisy Rose. "Would you like to come and live with your dad?"

Daisy Rose was squirming in her chair, no longer a precocious child, but a little girl who looked uneasy.

"Leave her alone," Sylvie ordered.

Shane pointedly ignored her. "Would you like to come live with your dad?" he repeated.

Daisy Rose looked as if she were shrinking into herself. Her zest, the very essence that made her so much like her mother, evaporated before their eyes. Jefferson curbed the desire to pull the other man to his feet and drag him away so that he no longer posed a threat to Daisy Rose's peace of mind.

The little girl turned her wide eyes toward her mother. "Mama?"

Sylvie tucked her arm around her daughter's shoulders. "Don't worry, baby, you're not going anywhere." She looked defiantly at Shane.

"I'm her father." Shane raised his voice. "I have some rights."

"Daisy Rose, would you take Emily out to the courtyard and show her the swimming pool?" Jefferson asked. He looked at Emily. "She just got here and she hasn't seen it yet."

Because she sensed Daisy Rose's mounting distress, Emily dutifully played along. "Please?" she said to the child.

"Okay." Hopping off her chair, Daisy Rose took Emily's hand and guided her over to the French doors leading out to the courtyard.

Sylvie shot Jefferson a grateful look. She waited until her daughter and Emily were out of earshot before resuming the verbal battle. There was no way Shane was getting her daughter.

"Sorry, Shane, but this time it's not about you. It's

about Daisy Rose and what's best for her." She leaned closer, her teeth all but clenched as she kept her voice low. "And that doesn't include living with a drug addict."

"*Former* drug addict," he countered with alacrity. "I've been clean and sober for almost three years now. It's a matter of record," he added proudly. "Shows how serious I am about getting her back."

"To get her *back,* you would have to have *had* her at some point," Sylvie reminded him. "And you never wanted her."

"You never gave me a chance," he parried.

"Liar."

This was going to get ugly at any minute, Jefferson thought. "Custody battles," he cut in quietly, "usually end up being ruled in favor of the mother." He looked at Shane. "Especially when the father has made no effort to contribute any financial support."

Shane drew himself up, squaring his shoulders. "I gave her money for the kid."

Jefferson heard Sylvie's sharp intake of breath. He put his hand over hers, quieting her, without looking in her direction. Instead, he showed the other man the futility of his lies. "And you kept records of that?"

Trapped, Shane looked away. "No, but—"

"And your drug addiction," Jefferson continued in the same quiet, forceful tone. "You went into rehab to kick that?"

"No," Shane declared proudly, "I did it all on my own."

Jefferson honed in on the obvious. "So there's no record of that, either."

Shane's expression darkened. "No. Hey, look—"

"You can spend the time and money fighting this, Mr. Alexander. A lot of time and money," he emphasized. "But the odds are against you from the start. In the end, you'll wind up losing. The case and the money."

Shane's expression had turned malevolent. "What are you, some kind of hotshot lawyer?" he demanded.

"Actually, I am." Taking out a card, he placed it on the table and pushed it over to Shane. Nowhere on the card did it state that he was a corporate lawyer, only that he worked for the firm of Pierce, Donovan and Klein. Shane took the card and read it, then snorted as he tossed it back down on the table.

"And you're *her* lawyer?"

Jefferson smiled slowly. "Among other things, yes, I am."

For a moment, Jefferson thought that the other man was going to challenge him, or at least vent. Instead, he laughed, shaking his head.

"You've gotten sharper, Sylvie."

Still on her guard, she looked at him warily. "I've had to."

Disgruntled, Shane turned to the woman at his right. "You're too young to be a mother, anyway, Patty. What do you say we start you on something simple, luv? Like a pet bird?"

Patty rose to her feet, contempt on her pretty face. "You're a real loser, you know that, Shane?" With those words, she turned on her heel and hurried away.

"Hope you didn't spend too much money on those wedding invitations," Sylvie commented.

Shane shrugged. "Doesn't matter. It was all her money anyway."

She nodded. "Things are beginning to come together." He was marrying the girl for her money. Money had always been Shane's driving force, his god.

"Guess I'd better go, too. See what it'll take to make her come around." He paused as he rose from the table. "Any objections if I say goodbye to Daisy Rose?"

She wanted to say yes, that he should leave without a single glance in Daisy Rose's direction. But he *was* the girl's father. She couldn't be unreasonable. Besides, Emily was with her. Daisy Rose was safe.

"As long as it's just goodbye," Sylvie qualified.

He saluted, a cynical expression on his face. Then, under Sylvie's watchful eye, Shane made his way outside to Emily and Daisy Rose.

"I wonder if I just made a mistake," Sylvie murmured under her breath.

"He won't steal her," Jefferson told her. "Emily knows tae kwon do." When she looked at him quizzically, he explained, "I wanted to make sure she could take care of herself if I wasn't around."

"I'll have to remember that for Daisy Rose."

As they watched through the French doors, Shane stopped to say something to the little girl. But then he turned his attention to Emily. His entire stance changed. When the rocker tossed his streaked mane over his shoulder, Jefferson's parenting instincts kicked in.

CHAPTER FIFTEEN

IN AN INSTANT, Jefferson was moving across the restaurant and out the doors like a bullet.

Surprised, Sylvie quickly rose from the table and followed. "Jefferson? What's wrong?"

Jefferson didn't waste time with words. His entire focus was on reaching them before that poor excuse for a human being had an opportunity to put his hands on his little girl. He could see it coming, feel it coming. Emily had blossomed early and looked older than her years, and Shane Alexander was the type who preyed on young, impressionable females.

He didn't make it in time. Just before he could get to Emily, he saw the other man touching her. Granted, Shane had only placed a hand indolently on her shoulder, but it was a body part. The preening peacock had invaded her space. Instead of talking to Daisy Rose, Shane was putting the moves on Emily, Jefferson thought angrily.

"What room are you staying in? I could come up and give you a private concert," he heard Shane saying to Emily.

It took no imagination to figure out just what the bastard was suggesting.

"Hey, Alexander," Jefferson called to him.

"Yeah?"

The former guitarist for Lynx didn't have an opportunity to say anything else. His jaw came in contact with a closed fist. The next second, he was on the ground, stunned, hurting and more than a little humiliated.

"Stay away from her," Jefferson warned him, as Daisy Rose gravitated to her mother's side.

Emily looked less than happy about her father riding to her rescue. "Dad, I can take care of myself," she informed him haughtily.

"What was that all about?" Sylvie hissed against his ear as she scooped Daisy Rose into her arms. Not that Shane didn't deserve that and more, but this kind of a display wasn't exactly the best for business.

"About putting someone in his place," Jefferson replied, his voice calm again. "And being a father." Because he was and always would be a gentleman, Jefferson extended his hand to the downed musician. "In case it makes a difference, she's sixteen."

Shane looked at the hand warily, then accepted it. Back on his feet, he held his jaw, nursing it tenderly. "She looks older," he said sullenly.

"Well, now you know," Jefferson replied. His eyes were steely. "You might want to do yourself, and everyone else, a favor and leave."

Shane muttered something to himself, then withdrew. Sylvie was certain he was cursing them all.

Emily was looking at her father with wonder, and a tinge of admiration shimmered beneath her world-weary facade. "I didn't think guys like you got physical, Dad."

He winked, draping an arm around her shoulders long enough to draw her in and give her a quick, bracing hug. "Guys like me are full of surprises." And then he looked at his watch. It was getting late. School had let out and by now Sophie was undoubtedly wondering where Emily was. "Let's go call your grandmother and tell her where you are. She's probably letting her imagination run away with her. And for once, her imagination isn't going to do this situation justice." Emily had the good grace to blush. Grinning, Jefferson looked at Sylvie. "Will you be at the gallery later?"

The gallery. With its empty space. How long could she stall before she absolutely had to go to her family—and the police? What if she was too late? She could keep the gallery closed for today, citing some vague excuse connected to the blackout. But what about tomorrow? Oh, God, life was getting too complicated for her.

Shifting Daisy Rose to her other hip, she nodded. "Yes."

He placed a hand at Emily's back to escort her toward the hotel. "I'll see you there, then."

It wasn't a vague statement, it was a promise, Sylvie realized. He meant what he'd said about helping her.

"Okay," Sylvie heard herself murmuring.

Hope, right now, was not springing eternal, but it had found a small toehold in her life. After all, Jefferson had just helped her eliminate Shane as a threat by posing as her lawyer. Maybe he could help her with the stolen painting.

He sure couldn't help her with her third problem, she thought, since he was the cause of it.

"I like him."

Daisy Rose's small, firm voice brought her back around to the moment. It took Sylvie a second to process the words and sentiment. She set her daughter back on the ground. It amazed her how uncomplicated life was through the eyes of a child. Daisy Rose was not afraid to make attachments. Sylvie envied the little girl. And maybe, she added silently, she could learn from her, as well.

"Yeah," Sylvie murmured under her breath. She could see Jefferson heading toward the elevators with his daughter. Everything about them said they cared about each other, through thick and thin. You had to admire a man who loved his daughter that way, who earned that kind of love from his daughter. *Love*. The word shimmered before her. Taunting. Tickling. "Me, too." And, if she were being honest with herself, that scared her. A lot.

EMILY GLANCED over her shoulder at mother and daughter, still standing by the pool. "She's pretty."

Jefferson nodded as he pressed for the elevator. "Yes, she is."

There was nothing but innocence in Emily's eyes as she asked, "Do you like her?"

Jefferson glanced at his daughter in surprise. "Emily…" It was meant as a warning, telling her to back off.

Instead, Emily dug in. A small flash of impatience crossed her face. She took after her mother there, he thought.

"It's not that complicated a question, Dad. Yes or no."

"On the contrary," he countered. "Questions like that are always complicated. The *subject* is complicated."

Emily sighed. "Stop being a lawyer, Dad. Just tell me. Yes, or no?"

The elevator arrived and he ushered her inside. Mercifully, after the car emptied out they were alone for the short ride up to the third floor. His logical side said it was much too soon for that sort of pronouncement. But there was another side—a side that Sylvie had drawn out of him—that had a different opinion.

"Yes."

Emily nodded as if she'd already come to a similar conclusion. "So, what are you going to do about it?"

He stared at her as if she had just lapsed into an unfamiliar language. "Do about it?" he echoed.

"Yes, do about it," she repeated. With dating skills like this, it was a wonder he'd ever connected with her mother, Emily thought.

The doors opened again and they were on his floor. "I'm going to enjoy it while I'm here."

There was too much finality in that to please Emily. She didn't relish the idea of going back to square one. "And then you're going to go home?"

Jefferson led the way to his suite. "That was always the plan."

Emily moved in front of him, walking backward so that she could face her father while presenting her argument. "But that was before you met Sylvie. Before you punched out her ex-lover."

He stopped at his door. Where had this dramatic flare come from? he wondered. Emily had always been so level-headed. "I hit him because he was coming on to you, Emily," he reminded her.

She was willing to concede that, if he was willing to concede that she was right, as well. "Yeah, but you also hit him because he got you mad. Because he was Sylvie's ex and he was making things difficult for her." Her grin grew wider. "You were a tiger back there, Dad. Don't you want to be a tiger again?"

After unlocking the door, he held it open for her. "Where is all this coming from?"

Emily walked in and glanced around. As far as rooms went, this looked like a homey one. She liked the blue and white bedspread. "The heart, Dad. You know, I'm not always going to be sixteen."

They had had this conversation before. "Yes, believe it or not, I do know that."

Her frown told him that she was ignoring his

sarcasm. But she pressed on. "And that means that you need to get a life of your own so that I don't feel guilty about having one of mine."

He struggled to hide his amusement. "Have you been watching Dr. Phil again?"

Emily rolled her eyes. "This is just common sense, Dad. I don't want you to be alone."

It was hard keeping a straight face. "When the time comes, I'll get a cat," he promised.

"You're allergic to cats," she reminded him. "I like Sylvie. She seems cool."

He agreed silently. But it was one thing for him to be contemplating a future with Sylvie, another for his daughter to be drawing up blueprints for it. Besides, he didn't want her disappointed if things didn't turn out.

"You don't know anything about her," he pointed out. "*I* don't know anything about her."

The objection was a trivial one to Emily and she waved it away. "Did you kiss her?"

When had their positions reversed? He gave her a look that told her she'd gone a little too far. "That is none of your business."

Emily nodded, drawing her own conclusions from his answer. "Okay, you kissed her." And then a sly, wicked look slipped over her face. "Maybe even more—"

Jefferson stared at his daughter. He had a good relationship with Emily, but that kind of information had no place in it. "Emily!"

Unfazed, she kept to her point. "And that means

that you know about as much as you need to about Sylvie." She shrugged nonchalantly. "The rest you can learn along the way." She crossed to the window and looked down onto the courtyard. It was charming. Everything about this place was charming, especially the fact that there wasn't any snow.

"I always wanted to live in New Orleans. Mom used to tell me the greatest stories about it." Turning from the window, she said, "And Grandma misses living here. She only came up to Boston because of Mom and then stayed after Mom died because of you and me. If we moved here, she'd be back in a heartbeat. She still thinks of this as home. We could keep the family intact—and expand it."

"Wouldn't you miss your friends?" he asked, once he ceased being stunned.

There was no particular boy in her life and she saw this as a huge adventure. "I could still visit once in a while, and so could they. Besides—" she grinned "—I'm resilient. I'd make new ones."

"You're taking an awful lot of things for granted, Emily. Adults don't move that fast."

"Maybe they should." She paused. Knowing her father, he was probably worried about providing for her. She didn't see that as a problem, either. "I'm sure you could get work here. You're too good not to."

Picking up the receiver, he held it out to her. "Call your grandmother."

She took the receiver, still looking at him. "And we'll discuss what I just said later?"

"Later," he echoed. *Much later.*

SYLVIE STARED at the wall in disbelief, feeling like someone who had just walked into the Twilight Zone.

It was back.

The painting was back.

She hadn't been able to get back to the gallery for almost an hour. What she'd been doing, after entrusting Daisy Rose to Melanie, was watching Shane and Patty, his just-this-side-of-legal-age, possible wife-to-be, check out. They'd been arguing, their voices growing louder as they departed.

All she cared about was that they were gone. She would have offered the hotel limousine to take them to the airport if it meant that Shane would leave sooner. Once the dueling couple had gone through the revolving doors, she had breathed a sigh of relief.

At least one threat, the most important one, was gone. From all appearances, she didn't have to worry about a custody battle over Daisy Rose. Jefferson had put the fear of God into Shane, who had neither the money nor the patience for a long, drawn-out court fight. If he couldn't get something by snapping his fingers, he lost interest. And anyone looking at him could see that the man had never had any real interest in being a father. The only reason he'd been here in the first place was to please his fiancée, who apparently was well off.

One problem gone, another to deal with….

The painting.

She'd walked into the gallery, mentally rehearsing what she would say to her grandmother. Heading straight for the empty wall, she found it wasn't empty anymore.

Shaken, still staring at the brilliant colors in the Wyeth, Sylvie sank down on the small bench she'd strategically placed before it so that visitors could sit and drink in its beauty and tranquility. A feast for the eye. The crate containing the two paintings she'd loaned Maddy had arrived within the past hour and Luc, bless him, had taken the delivery, verified that the paintings were in fact there, even offered to hang them for her.

She'd hesitated, then given her permission. She'd been bracing herself for some comment from him when she'd returned to the gallery. Surprised to find that the doors were once again locked, she'd opened the one that led from the hotel lobby and walked in.

To see this.

The three paintings were hanging exactly the way they had been before she'd taken the two larger ones down for Maddy.

Sylvie sighed, shaking her head. Had she just imagined the whole thing? Had she been so shaken up, her world so completely rocked last night by Jefferson that she'd begun hallucinating and just imagined her grandmother's Wyeth was missing?

No, Jefferson knew that the painting was missing—that it had been taken. He'd been the one to ask if she wanted him to call the police.

She wanted to ask Luc if the painting was there when he'd hung up the others, but she didn't know how to do that without raising his suspicions. Maybe someone had just taken it as a Twelfth Night prank.

Taking a deep breath, she ran her hand through her hair. Sylvie felt light-headed, almost to the point of passing out. She wondered if this was what having a nervous breakdown was like.

But then, if she was having a nervous breakdown, would she feel like singing? And she'd felt like singing since this morning.

Deal in realities.

The reality was that the painting was exactly where it was supposed to be and so was Daisy Rose. She should have felt like celebrating three times over. What else could she possibly ask for?

You know what else you could ask for, a small voice whispered in her head.

She did her best to shut it out, telling herself not to be greedy.

IT SEEMED TO LUC that he was never going to breathe normally again. Especially if his heart didn't settle down.

He'd managed to do it just in time. Return the painting back to its original spot a few minutes before Sylvie walked in.

He took a second to savor the moment. His conscience had been bothering him since the minute he had the painting in his possession. But he had to admit that what tipped the scales for him was his keen sense of survival. Being caught with the painting would have severely interfered with that.

Causing a few small items to disappear—none of the things he'd taken from the various rooms were of any real value—came under the heading of nuisance. But the Wyeth, well, that was grand theft. A very real, very long prison sentence would be attached to a conviction.

It wasn't something he was willing to chance, especially when he was no longer certain about the course he was on. It was just too risky. If anyone had found the painting…

Luc didn't finish the thought. Dan and Richard weren't going to be happy with him. But then, they wouldn't have been the ones doing time if he had been caught.

It was better this way, he thought. There were other ways to make waves. And he needed to come up with one fast, to get the Corbin brothers off his back.

SYLVIE LOOKED at Jefferson, a thousand emotions raging through her—scrambling, tangling, making both her heart and her head ache. She'd never been happier—or sadder—in her life. How was that possible? Unless, of course, she was in—

Was that it? she thought suddenly, surprised. Was this what being in love was all about? Thrilled at the possibility, yet terrified of losing it at the same time? Terrified on so many levels?

And happy on even more. She sighed, but it was a joyful sound.

After Celeste's painting was back in its place and Shane Alexander had returned to the hole he'd crawled out of, it still wasn't business as usual for her.

Far from it, she mused, trailing her fingers down Jefferson's bare arm. He had placed his concerned daughter on a plane bound for Boston and had remained to attend his fraternity reunion. Had remained to weave himself into her life in the space of five days. Five days that had gone by much too fast.

And this was the last night. She'd attended the final reunion gala with him, trying to absorb every moment, every word he said, every expression. Praying that somehow the evening wouldn't end.

But it had. And now they were in his hotel room.

In his bed.

She'd made a resolution to remain strong, to walk away from him at the end of the evening with dignity. She'd had no intention of being here with him like this.

But then an annoying little voice had whispered, *Why not? This might be the last time you'll be together. Why not stay? Why not make love?*

Why not indeed.

So she had. And they did. They'd made love as if this would be the last time. As if the world were coming to an end in the morning. In a way, for her, it was.

Trying very hard to be brave, Sylvie now forced the words to her lips. Words she felt were expected of her. She stared at the ceiling instead of at Jefferson, thinking if she did the latter, she would cry.

"I'll drive you to the airport in the morning."

She felt Jefferson shifting beside her. "About that…" he began.

She didn't want to hear it. Rising up on her elbow, she looked at him. "If you've made other plans, cancel them," she ordered.

Amusement played over his lips. Was he laughing at her?

"Are you sure you want me to do that?"

She raised her chin, struggling to control nerves that were suddenly, unaccountably, fraying. "I just said so, didn't I?"

The look on his face was unreadable. "Don't you even want to hear what my other plan is?"

Why would she want to do that? "What? A taxi? Your friend Blake? That carriage you commandeered the night of the blackout?"

"No," he replied quietly, running his finger along the curve of her neck, "my other plan is not to leave."

Stunned, she stared at him. "What?"

"Well," he explained, "not in the permanent sense." He would have to fly back to Boston, to make arrangements. To tie up loose ends. To pack.

She wasn't following. "Is this some of that lawyer double-talk?"

"No, straight talk," he promised. He wasn't good at teasing. "I've been thinking that maybe it's time for me to move back here. Emily said she wanted to, and the best years of my life have their roots right here." His eyes held hers for a moment. "I think they might again."

Excitement and joy vibrated within her. She was

afraid to hope, but wanted to desperately. "You're going to live here? Really?"

Jefferson smiled but held himself in check, wanting nothing more than to sweep her back into his arms and make love with her all over again. That would be setting a record, he realized. His own personal best. She did that: she brought out the best in him.

"I take it that doesn't meet with your disapproval?"

It sounded too good to be true, Sylvie thought.

"But what will you do?" she asked.

"I renewed a few friendships at the reunion tonight. Seems there's an opening at one of the major firms here. I know the senior partner. As a matter of fact, he made me an offer that's quite attractive."

Sylvie didn't remember hearing any talk of offers. Was he just making this up? Teasing her for some reason? "When?"

Jefferson grinned. He could almost see the thoughts scooting across her mind. "When you went to powder your nose."

She scrutinized his expression, looking for a sign that he was joking. But there was none. "Then you're serious?"

"Very." Knowing the value of a well-placed pause, he made use of it now before continuing. "Oh, there's one more thing."

Here it comes, she thought. The bombshell. She braced herself for disappointment. "What?"

Jefferson wrapped his arm around her, bringing her closer to him. "Will you marry me?"

Okay, now she was sure of it. She was dreaming.

On the small outside chance that she wasn't, Sylvie softly asked, "What?"

"Will you marry me?" he repeated even more earnestly than the first time.

He was going to regret this, she thought. "But you don't know me," she protested.

"I know everything I need to about you." Emily, he thought, was right. That girl was wise beyond her years, but he was still going to keep a watchful eye on her. "That I love you. I knew the first time I looked at Emily's mother that she was the one for me. I felt the same thing when I looked at you." Because the thought had scared him, he fought it. But now he knew this was the right thing to do. This was the right woman for him.

He smiled into her eyes, stopping only to kiss her softly before going on. "I'm never wrong when it comes to things like this. We don't have to get married right away. It can be a long courtship. Say, six months or so if you like. It'll take that long to get everything squared away in Boston. I'd want Emily to finish school…" He grew serious, realizing how much her answer meant to him. How much he feared hearing the wrong one. "I realize that this is sudden and you're going to need some time to think things through, but—"

"Yes." The single word burst from her lips.

He raised a brow. "Yes?"

"Yes," she cried.

"You don't want any time to think about it?"

"I *have* been thinking about it," she confessed. "Thinking about it ever since you kissed me. And in case you're wondering, I love you, too. And Daisy Rose talks about you all the time."

His eyes grew soft as he brought her mouth back to his.

"Good," he replied. "Very good."

And it was.

HOTEL MARCHAND
Four sisters.
A family legacy.
And someone is out to destroy it.

There's a dead woman in Matt Anderson's
hotel room and he has no idea
how she got there.
When Kerry Johnston appears from
next door to help, both she and Matt
recognize the woman as a local waitress and
practitioner of voodoo.
That's all *anyone* seems to know about her,
but it's not enough for Matt and Kerry.

Here's a preview!

He quickly walked the few blocks to the hotel. His heart felt much lighter as he entered the courtyard from the alley. Odd, he thought, how you could meet someone and suddenly life seemed better....

He spotted Kerry seated at a table under an umbrella, talking to two women. He headed toward her.

"Hello," she said upon seeing him, her manner so full of welcome it was all he could do to keep from crushing her against him and holding her, just holding her.

Cool it, some saner part of him cautioned. While Kerry seemed the embodiment of all his dreams, he wasn't going to lose his head over any woman.

"Good afternoon," he said to all three women.

"You've met Charlotte," Kerry continued, "and this is her mother, Anne Marchand. I was just telling them about Patti's cremation and our plans for tomorrow."

Matt shook hands with the older woman, who was around sixty, he estimated, but looked younger and was in fact a very attractive woman. By contrast her daughter seemed tired and stressed, as if she hadn't slept well lately.

Since Saturday night, he was willing to bet. His gaze went to Kerry, who looked bright and alert and, okay, *wholesome* in slacks and sweater that showed off her curves to perfection. It seemed to Matt she grew more beautiful each time he saw her.

"Join us," Kerry invited, smiling up at him.

He sat in the vacant chair between Kerry and Anne.

"I must tell you that I'm surprised at what you two are doing for that unfortunate young woman," Anne said, looking from one to the other. She shook her head. "You are living proof of the kindness of strangers."

A silence, tense with sadness, ensued. Kerry's eyes were moist, Matt noticed.

"I stopped by the crematorium," he told her, his tone gentle. "Everything is going as planned."

She laid a hand on his arm, her eyes on him as if he'd done some heroic deed. "Thank you, Matt. That's a load off my mind." She turned to the two women. "We're going to find her former home and scatter her ashes there."

"The detective said she listed no next of kin at the restaurant where she worked," Charlotte mentioned.

"Kerry and I did some sleuthing and found out where she was from," Matt said. "There was once a family plantation." He turned to look at Kerry. "It's not far from Lafayette. If we leave between nine and ten in the morning, we should have plenty of time. I've arranged for a rental car."

Kerry pressed the heel of her hand to her forehead. "Oh, I didn't think about transportation and all that. Yes, let's leave early and get it over with."

"You two haven't had a vacation at all," Anne protested. "You're using your time to help others."

Charlotte nodded. "I agree. It so happens there have been a few cancellations since Saturday." She smiled at the couple. "Won't you stay another week as our guests? That seems only fair. Or if that isn't possible, then you must return another time and give us a chance to make your stay here as pleasant—and uneventful—as it should be."

"That's very kind of you," Kerry said. "I could stay over a couple of days. I didn't schedule any appointments until next Thursday in order to have a few days to settle in before I return to work. How about you?"

When she glanced at Matt, he nodded agreement. "I'll be writing an article based on my research in the city. I can do it here as well as in New York."

"Wonderful," Anne said, rising and wishing them all a good day.

Charlotte paused after her mother left them. "Please have dinner as our guests this evening. In fact, all your meals will be comped. I insist," she added when Matt and Kerry assured her they expected no such thing.

"Well," Matt said when he was alone with Kerry, "my publisher will be pleased. My expense account should be much lower than expected on this trip."

"What about the rental car?" she asked.

"That's a personal expense," he said, "something I want to do. With you."

Her eyes widened, then gleamed with pleasure. "Me, too," she said softly.

Matt's heart set off again. That old black magic of legend and song had them in its spell, it seemed.

Funny, but in this case, he didn't mind. Being attracted to Kerry was fun. As long as he didn't do anything stupid like think he was falling in love.

REQUEST YOUR FREE BOOKS!

2 FREE NOVELS
FROM THE SUSPENSE COLLECTION
PLUS 2 FREE GIFTS!

YES! Please send me 2 FREE novels from the Suspense Collection and my 2 FREE gifts (gifts are worth about $10). After receiving them, if I don't wish to receive any more books, I can return the shipping statement marked "cancel." If I don't cancel, I will receive 3 brand-new novels every month and be billed just $5.74 per book in the U.S. or $6.24 per book in Canada. That's a savings of at least $2.25 off the cover price. It's quite a bargain! Shipping and handling is just 50¢ per book.* I understand that accepting the 2 free books and gifts places me under no obligation to buy anything. I can always return a shipment and cancel at any time. Even if I never buy another book from the Reader Service, the two free books and gifts are mine to keep forever.

192 MDN EZQ7 392 MDL EZRK

Name _____ (PLEASE PRINT) _____

Address _____ Apt. # _____

City _____ State/Prov. _____ Zip/Postal Code _____

Signature (if under 18, a parent or guardian must sign)

Mail to **The Reader Service:**
IN U.S.A.: P.O. Box 1867, Buffalo, NY 14240-1867
IN CANADA: P.O. Box 609, Fort Erie, Ontario L2A 5X3

Not valid to current subscribers of the Suspense Collection
or the Romance/Suspense Collection.

Want to try two free books from another line?
Call 1-800-873-8635 or visit www.morefreebooks.com.

* Terms and prices subject to change without notice. Prices do not include applicable taxes. Sales tax applicable in N.Y. Canadian residents will be charged applicable provincial taxes and GST. Offer not valid in Quebec. This offer is limited to one order per household. All orders subject to approval. Credit or debit balances in a customer's account(s) may be offset by any other outstanding balance owed by or to the customer. Please allow 4 to 6 weeks for delivery. Offer available while quantities last.

Your Privacy: Harlequin is committed to protecting your privacy. Our Privacy Policy is available online at www.eHarlequin.com or upon request from the Reader Service. From time to time we make our lists of customers available to reputable third parties who may have a product or service of interest to you. If you would prefer we not share your name and address, please check here. ☐

MSUS09HM

REQUEST YOUR
FREE BOOKS!

2 FREE NOVELS
FROM THE ROMANCE COLLECTION
PLUS 2 FREE GIFTS!

YES! Please send me 2 FREE novels from the Romance Collection and my 2 FREE gifts (gifts are worth about $10). After receiving them, if I don't wish to receive any more books, I can return the shipping statement marked "cancel." If I don't cancel, I will receive 3 brand-new novels every month and be billed just $5.74 per book in the U.S. or $6.24 per book in Canada. That's a savings of at least $2.25 off the cover price. It's quite a bargain! Shipping and handling is just 50¢ per book.* I understand that accepting the 2 free books and gifts places me under no obligation to buy anything. I can always return a shipment and cancel at any time. Even if I never buy another book from the Reader Service, the two free books and gifts are mine to keep forever.

193 MDN EZQK   393 MDN EZQV

Name _____ (PLEASE PRINT)

Address _____ Apt. #

City _____ State/Prov. _____ Zip/Postal Code

Signature (if under 18, a parent or guardian must sign)

Mail to **The Reader Service:**
IN U.S.A.: P.O. Box 1867, Buffalo, NY 14240-1867
IN CANADA: P.O. Box 609, Fort Erie, Ontario L2A 5X3

Not valid to current subscribers of the Romance Collection
or the Romance/Suspense Collection.

Want to try two free books from another line?
Call 1-800-873-8635 or visit www.morefreebooks.com.

* Terms and prices subject to change without notice. Prices do not include applicable taxes. Sales tax applicable in N.Y. Canadian residents will be charged applicable provincial taxes and GST. Offer not valid in Quebec. This offer is limited to one order per household. All orders subject to approval. Credit or debit balances in a customer's account(s) may be offset by any other outstanding balance owed by or to the customer. Please allow 4 to 6 weeks for delivery. Offer available while quantities last.

Your Privacy: Harlequin is committed to protecting your privacy. Our Privacy Policy is available online at www.eHarlequin.com or upon request from the Reader Service. From time to time we make our lists of customers available to reputable third parties who may have a product or service of interest to you. If you would prefer we not share your name and address, please check here. ☐

MROM09HM

REQUEST YOUR FREE BOOKS!

2 FREE NOVELS PLUS 2 FREE GIFTS!

HARLEQUIN®

Super Romance®

Exciting, emotional, unexpected!

YES! Please send me 2 FREE Harlequin® Superromance® novels and my 2 FREE gifts (gifts are worth about $10). After receiving them, if I don't wish to receive any more books, I can return the shipping statement marked "cancel." If I don't cancel, I will receive 6 brand-new novels every month and be billed just $4.69 per book in the U.S. or $5.24 per book in Canada. That's a savings of close to 15% off the cover price! It's quite a bargain! Shipping and handling is just 50¢ per book*. I understand that accepting the 2 free books and gifts places me under no obligation to buy anything. I can always return a shipment and cancel at any time. Even if I never buy another book from Harlequin, the two free books and gifts are mine to keep forever.

135 HDN EZRV   336 HDN EZR7

Name _____ (PLEASE PRINT) _____

Address _____ Apt. # _____

City _____ State/Prov. _____ Zip/Postal Code _____

Signature (if under 18, a parent or guardian must sign) _____

Mail to the **Harlequin Reader Service:**
IN U.S.A.: P.O. Box 1867, Buffalo, NY 14240-1867
IN CANADA: P.O. Box 609, Fort Erie, Ontario L2A 5X3

Not valid to current subscribers of Harlequin Superromance books.

**Are you a current subscriber of Harlequin Superromance books
and want to receive the larger-print edition?
Call 1-800-873-8635 today!**

* Terms and prices subject to change without notice. Prices do not include applicable taxes. Sales tax applicable in N.Y. Canadian residents will be charged applicable provincial taxes and GST. Offer not valid in Quebec. This offer is limited to one order per household. All orders subject to approval. Credit or debit balances in a customer's account(s) may be offset by any other outstanding balance owed by or to the customer. Please allow 4 to 6 weeks for delivery. Offer available while quantities last.

Your Privacy: Harlequin is committed to protecting your privacy. Our Privacy Policy is available online at www.eHarlequin.com or upon request from the Reader Service. From time to time we make our lists of customers available to reputable third parties who may have a product or service of interest to you. If you would prefer we not share your name and address, please check here. ☐

HSR09HM

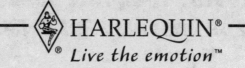

HARLEQUIN®
INTRIGUE®

BREATHTAKING ROMANTIC SUSPENSE

Shared dangers and passions lead to electrifying romance and heart-stopping suspense!

Every month, you'll meet six new heroes who are guaranteed to make your spine tingle and your pulse pound. With them you'll enter into the exciting world of Harlequin Intrigue— where your life is on the line and so is your heart!

THAT'S INTRIGUE—
ROMANTIC SUSPENSE
AT ITS BEST!

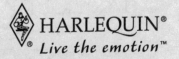

HARLEQUIN®
Live the emotion™

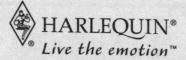

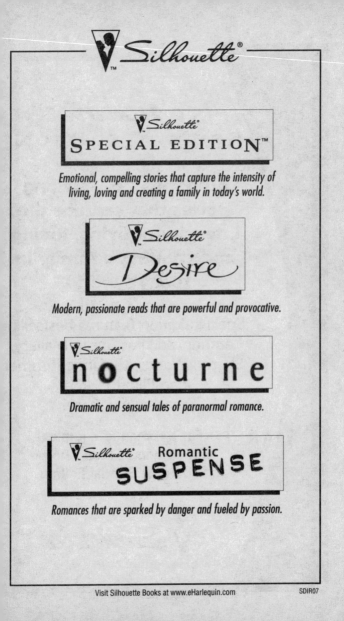

Silhouette®

▼ Silhouette®
SPECIAL EDITION™

Emotional, compelling stories that capture the intensity of living, loving and creating a family in today's world.

▼ Silhouette®
Desire

Modern, passionate reads that are powerful and provocative.

▼ Silhouette®
nocturne

Dramatic and sensual tales of paranormal romance.

▼ Silhouette® Romantic
SUSPENSE

Romances that are sparked by danger and fueled by passion.